D0640334

HOODS HOT RODS AND HELLCATS

EDITED BY CHAD EAGLETON

CATHODE ANGEL

Collection ©2013 Chad Eagleton
Introduction ©2013 Mick Farren
Individual stories ©2013 their respective authors.

All rights reserved. No part of this book may be reproduced in any form or by any means without written consent, except where permitted by law.

The stories contained herein are works of fiction. All the characters, places, and events are either products of the imagination or used fictitiously. Any resemblance to actual persons, living or dead, is entirely coincidental.

Cover Art © 2013 Skott Kilander
Spot Illustrations © 2013 Curtis Pierce
Cover design and Cathode Angel Logo by Brian S. Roe of RSquared Studios.

CONTENTS

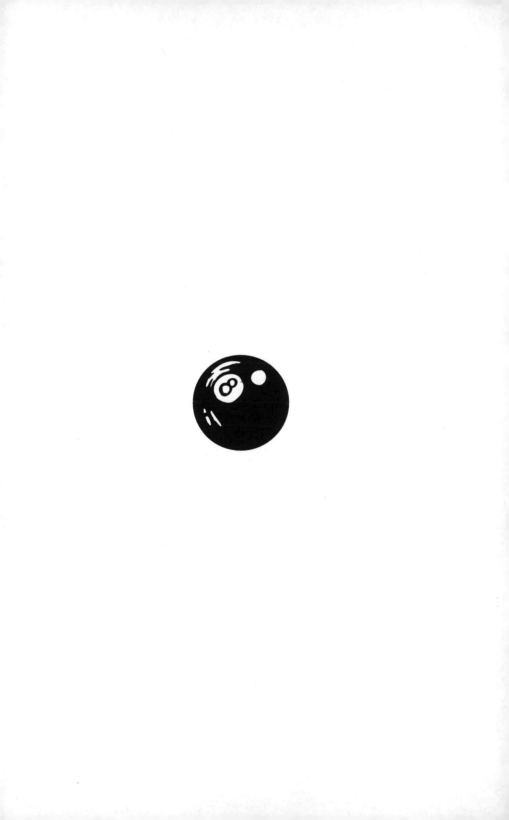

For my lovely wife.

INTRODUCTION

Like any fictional landscape—Wyatt Earp's Old West, the Arthurian Roundtable, Dracula's Transylvania, or Mike Hammer's concrete jungle—the world of *Hoods, Hot Rods, and Hellcats* is a dirty cocktail of fact, fable, fears, and fantasies. The 1950s are recreated one more time but here it's with a savage, razor-honed edge you'll never find in *Grease, Happy Days,* or *American Graffiti.*

The desolate dysfunction, the hard chaos, and the raw psychosis of the time are major ingredients rather than concealed truths. The switchblade snaps open and the word *Stiletto* is engraved on the blade to prove it's the real deal. The doomed desire of the homicidal lesbian outlaws in Christopher Grant's story "1958: Somewhere In Texas" was plainly lifted from the ultra-lurid cover art of trash paperback pulp fiction, but, at the same time, they are a wildly extended parable of 1950s sexual repression, homophobia, and emotionally stunted grey flannel prurience. This was the 1950s where Chuck Berry could be on American Bandstand doing the duck walk and singing about "Sweet Little Sixteen" in her "tight dresses and lipstick, wearing high-heeled shoes", but Chuck would also do hard jail time on trumped up charges of transporting Sweet Little Sixteen across the state line for the purposes of prostitution. And all because Chuck was too damned fond of white girls for Missouri law enforcement.

The USA in the aftermath of World War II was, to say the least, a confused superpower. It had emerged from the close-to-apocalyptic conflict not only victorious but with all the marbles. Atomic bombs had been developed in a shroud of secrecy and then used to vaporize two Japanese cities. Before the attack on Pearl Harbor, and the US entering the war, the nation had been clawing its way out of the Great Depression, mass unemployment, breadlines, and the Dust Bowl. Now the spoils of war had made America a promised land of milk and honey. The dilemma for those in power was how exactly that promise would be kept and how the milk and honey would be shared.

Wartime had forced a necessary uniformity on the country and for many politicians, industrialists, and power brokers it seemed like a mighty fine idea to impose a peacetime version of that same worker/consumer lockstep. They set out to design a world in which everyone thought alike, dressed alike, had the same haircuts, and drove variations of the same cars, straight out of Detroit. The goal was a docile population that watched the same TV shows, read the same books and magazines, and lived on suburban streets of near identical houses with their 2.5 children. The men went to work at the same offices and factories, while the women stayed home using all the shiny new homemaker gadgets and appliances—speeding the Hoover with the heavily marketed Dexedrine pills. They kept their houses spotless during the day and fucked like bunnies at night, if only out of amphetamine boredom—but that part was never talked about. And if the walls started to close in there were always Martinis, Marlboros and meprobamate. (Also known as Miltowns.)

The kids went to the same schools—racially segregated in the South—recited the Pledge of Allegiance and learned from a cartoon turtle called Bert how to hide under their classroom desks during an atomic attack. This free enterprise Utopia needed to be kept in line by thermonuclear fear of the Soviet Red Menace and its rockets on the other side of the world. The CIA even had a name for it—the psycho-civilized society. No place in there for hoods, hot rods, and hellcats. Fortunately around 1956, a young handsome malcontent called Elvis Presley sashayed out of Memphis public housing to upset this regimented applecart and lead a children's crusade to what Bob Dylan would later call the Gates of Eden.

Elvis wasn't the only cultural rebel of the time. He wasn't even the first; he was just the one who made it to the gold suit, the gold records, and Ed Sullivan, and reduced a million little girls across the planet to moist orgasmic hysteria. Elvis was simply playing to a reality that those in authority and their managed media refused to even acknowledge. A strain of postwar discontent was loose in the land. More war veterans than anyone cared to admit had trouble adjusting to this psycho-civilized society. Men who had hit the beaches on D-Day or crewed a B17 Flying Fortress weren't going to make an easy transition to clocking in as production line wage slaves, or stacking shelves in a supermarket. Escape from a suffocating civilian monotony frequently came on two wheels or four—a customized Hudson Hornet or a panhead Harley Davidson Hydra-Glide could provide a two-lane blacktop getaway and something akin to the adventure and adrenaline rush of combat. Veterans looking for the close bonds and camaraderie of wartime formed the first outlaw motorcycle clubs—the forerunners of the Hells Angels. And if that wasn't problem enough, many of these vets still suffered from Post-Traumatic Stress Disorder, which made them unpredictable and even dangerous—especially when drunk.

The image of the beer swilling, whiskey crazed hoodlum biker was crystallized in the public psyche in 1947 by what have become known as the Hollister riots when early clubs like The Pissed Off Bastards, The Boozefighters, and The Market Street Commandos—more than 4,000 in all—descended on the small town of Hollister, California for a weekend of motorized, alcohol-fueled fun and mayhem during which 50-60 bikers were injured and about the same number arrested. *The San Francisco Chronicle* and *Life Magazine* both played up the story. Lurid reporting and photography to shock the squares implanted the idea that hoodlum bikers were a clear and present danger to public order. Life and art began a circular jitterbug that mythologized the Hollister riots as the start of some much wider and wilder cultural evolution. In 1951 a short story in Harper's magazine based on Hollister—"The Cyclists' Raid" by Frank Rooney—provided the inspiration for the movie *The Wild One* and junior hoods began to acquire icons.

Brando and Lee Marvin, James Dean and Natalie Wood became role models for a generation without a cause. In the US and then all across the so-called Free World, teens talked the talk and walked the walk. "What are you rebelling against, Johnny?" Johnny Strabler doesn't have to think about it as he drums on the jukebox. "What've you got?" Young boys in London copied the way Marlon lit a cigarette, in Paris they reproduced the way he used his sunglasses. The black leather jacket and blue jeans became an ad hoc rebel uniform from Los Angeles to Tokyo. Girls took up the gun moll look—Susan Hayward in the film *I Want To Live*, playing the real life Barbara Graham who went to the San Quentin gas chamber, ratted out by one of her companions in a botched robbery. Other sweet sixteen hellcats copied the style with which Brigitte Bardot flaunted her obvious sexuality.

The resistance to enforced conformity spread and grew and was readily exploited by cheap-and-sleazy, bargain-basement media. It wasn't that a cohesive 1950s underground was coagulating. That would take another decade and the Vietnam War. It was more that unconnected but related blows were being struck against the empire with increasing frequency. Car clubs, street racers, lowriders, biker clubs and urban street gangs were sensationalized in the press and on TV as a menacing juvenile delinquent underworld. Kick-ass, wild-man rockers like Gene Vincent and Jerry Lee Lewis—who, in real life had frequently to skip town after a show, one jump ahead of the Sheriff, with their booze, pills and proto-groupies—were cast in low budget teen exploitation movies like *Hot Rod Gang* and *High School Confidential*.

Bettie Page became a fetish goddess in a plain brown wrapper. EC comics catered to universal teen ghoulishness with titles like *Vault of Horror* and *Tales From The Crypt*, and the authorities stamped hard on both Bettie and EC.

Salvador Agron was more than stamped on. He only narrowly missed the Sing Sing electric chair. One of a Brooklyn gang called The Vampires; he stabbed two teenagers to death in an ill-conceived gang fight. In the media frenzy that surrounded his trial, he was dubbed "The Capeman" because he wore a black cape with a red lining over his leathers for the fight. When arrested he reportedly snarled at the cops, "I don't care if I burn, my mother could watch me!"

Agron may have dodged execution, but Charles Starkweather actually went to the chair. Charlie Starkweather—a James Dean look-a-like from Lincoln Nebraska—and his underage gun moll squeeze Caril Fugate went on a two-month hot rod slay spree that claimed eleven victims. The country was shocked. Starkweather conformed to the popular Hollywood image of the teen psycho to the point of declaring his philosophy "Dead people are all on the same level", and he would inspire the films *Badlands* and *Natural Born Killers*, and the Bruce Springsteen album *Nebraska*. In Chad Eagleton's story "Blue Jeans and a Boy's Shirt" the character Daisy describes Starkweather and Fugate as "Two lonely and broken people who found each other and were happy for a moment and crushed whatever threatened it." The fictional Daisy not only sums up the poignancy, but also the pain of individualism in a straightjacket mass culture. *Hoods, Hot Rods, and Hellcats* is, at root, about escape. Escape in the '49 Ford, navigating the back-roads of what Jim Morrison would call a "desperate land."

Needless to say, the pulp fiction industry was quick to jump on the teen hoodlum bandwagon. Paperback titles with gorgeously lurid covers like *The Young Wolves*, *Rock 'N Roll Gal*, *Hot Rod Rumble*, and *Gang Girls* rolled off the presses and joined the hard-boiled detective, the space opera, and semi-porn sex novels on the drugstore bookrack. Science fiction master Harlan Ellison joined the genre early in his career with a novel called *Rumble*, but the real star of teen sex, speed, and violence literature was the late Hal Ellson whose books *Tomboy*, *Duke*, *Jailbait Street*, and *A Nest Of Fear* are now sought-after collector's items. The unexpected truth is *Hoods, Hot Rods, and Hellcats* not only has a complex social history but also is part of a noble and valued literary tradition. Who'd have thought it?

~Mick Farren, Brighton 2013

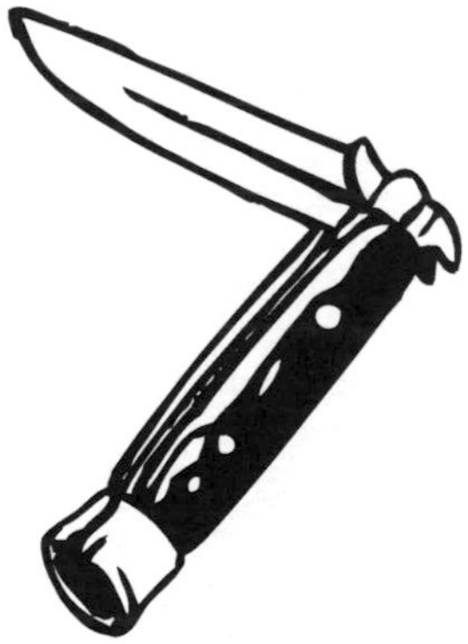

1958: SOMEWHERE IN TEXAS
CHRISTOPHER GRANT

NOVEMBER:

I met Jane when we were both seventeen. It was the last year of high school. I had still not decided what I was going to do once I graduated and didn't have a hell of a lot of options.

After Jane and I graduated, I met Delores on a weekend drive into southern Oklahoma.

The differences between the three of us were balanced by the similarities. Jane and I were lovers for nearly six months by the time we met Delores.

Delores thought that we were both going to hell, being lesbians and all that.

I noticed that she never said anything about the other shit that we did. The robberies and the killing and all that shit.

Maybe because she didn't want to include herself in that trip to Hades. Good little Christian Delores would be forgiven her sins but not Jane and definitely not me.

It's part of the reason I shot Delores first. Actually, it's only the tip of the iceberg.

EARLY-JUNE:

Graduation is next week. Prom is tonight.

Jane and I have been having sex with each other for a couple of weeks now.

Jane didn't even bother trying to hide her attraction to me. Told me that she liked me more than any of the other girls in school. She asked me if she could kiss me.

My heart was beating through my chest, beating through my blouse, remembering the Polaroid photos and wondering if it will be like that.

I nodded, and she kissed me. It wasn't any different than kissing a boy, though I hadn't kissed a boy since I was twelve and Tommy, a kid in the neighborhood, told me that he liked me. So I kissed him.

Prom is supposed to be the night that you remember the rest of your life.

I know I will.

Jane and I show up together and the first word that I hear is dyke.

And I know exactly who's saying it, too.

Tommy.

I wait for the right moment during the night, and then I pull Tommy aside. Believe it or not, despite the comment, he actually comes outside with me.

"Remember when we were twelve and you told me you liked me?" I say.

We're sitting on the stairs in front of our high school.

"When did you figure that you liked pussy instead?" he says.

We're both smoking. I grin with the cigarette between my teeth and open the Zippo lighter that I stole from my father.

I pull the cigarette from my mouth and put it out in his eye. While he struggles with the pain and the sudden blindness, I touch the lit wick to Tommy's sleeve, and then bend forward and touch it on the cuff of his pants. It all happens so fast, too fast for him to do anything about it.

Fuck you, too, Tommy, I think, as I watch him burn.

APRIL:

Mom and Dad are out of town for the weekend. I invite one of the girls from school, Jane, over to stay with me. Sometimes, not all the time, but sometimes, I get afraid at night.

Before she comes over, I go exploring the house.

It's strange what you notice when you're allowed to look without someone over your shoulder.

I never knew that we had an attic. I always thought that the panel that is the entrance to the attic was just a misshaped panel, nothing more. Never noticed that there's a string to pull it open.

When the little staircase pops out, I jump back and laugh at my fear of some stupid little stairs. I climb the stairs into the attic and immediately have to duck to avoid hitting my head on one of the low-hanging beams. Slowly, I pick my way across the attic, careful of where I step, still stooped over.

Boxes full of things forgotten. I find the cloth doll my aunt made me when I was five, brush cobwebs off her yarn hair.

Books in one of the boxes. Old books, new books.

Lurid covers on some of the books.

I flip through others, and there are cartoons having sex. Most of them female cartoons having sex with female cartoons.

The books with the lurid covers are about women being attracted to other women, too. Random passages about unnatural feelings, feelings that eventually are given into.

In one of the paperbacks, I find a Polaroid. I drop it as if it has singed my fingers. I pick it up and see two women kissing, fondling each other. These are real, flesh and blood women, not like those depicted on the covers of the paperbacks. I feel a flutter in my stomach as if I'm about to be sick. At the same time, I cannot deny that I feel turned on. I leaf through every paperback and cannot find another photo. I look through the other boxes and find what I'm looking for. More photos of these same women, in various sexual positions.

And then, as I continue to look through the photos, there is a man with these women, watching them, and then joining them.

The man is my father.

There is a faint knock on the door, the attic keeping it from being louder. I wonder how long she's been there.

I come out of the attic and down the staircase to answer the door.

Jane, blonde and beautiful, is standing there, an ear-to-ear smile on her face.

"I need to show you something," I say to her. I don't know why. It just slips out. I take her by the hand and lead her to the attic.

EARLY-JULY:

The investigation into what happened to Tommy Elder concludes very simply: I was defending myself while he attempted to rape me.

This is what I told the police.

And, after a handful of weeks, they finally believe me.

Doesn't matter that it's not the truth or that a number of people in town don't believe me or that Tommy's friends and family think I should go to the death chamber for killing their friend/son/brother.

It's the police that matter and the district attorney, and neither of them think that I should face charges.

Jane stands by me the entire time.

When it's all over, she asks me for the first time, "None of that was true, was it? Tommy didn't really try to rape you, did he?"

"No," I say. I can't lie to her.

"Cool," Jane says and kisses me.

NOVEMBER, BACK IN TEXAS:

The shack is where we meet up. We've been traveling here in separate cars because the heat is too heavy for three women traveling together. I've gone to the lengths of peroxiding my hair. Jane is wearing a black wig. Delores has cut her hair short.

Delores is already there when I get to the shack.

"It's good to be home," she says to me. "I missed this."

I laugh to myself. How can she call this home? She wasn't even born in Texas. How could she have missed this? She wasn't even with us when Jane and I killed the guy from the bar.

I pull out my father's Zippo and light a cigarette. I don't bother offering Delores one. She doesn't smoke anyway.

She's got her eyes closed and sits in the rocking chair in the center of the only room in the twelve-by-ten foot shack.

I hear Jane finally pull up outside as I reach into the back of my waistband and feel the cool steel of the Saturday Night pistol there.

If I time this right, I'll get the result that I want.

LATE-MAY:

Mom and Dad go out of town for an Army reunion. Dad served in the Big One. He was in Europe in late-'44 and a little bit of '45. My earliest memory of him is when he came home from the war and we threw him a grand old party. I was four.

Mom tries her best to convince me to come along. I tell her that I don't want to miss any of the graduation parties the other parents are throwing their kids. It's almost a guilt trip that I'm playing but I have other reasons for not going, not the least of which is the discovery in the attic.

I used to think of my father as respectable. All he ever talked about was personal responsibility. His hard-ass attitude, inherited from my grandfather and beaten into him by the military, is stark contrast to those photos.

"Have you seen my Zippo?" My father asks me. I shake my head side to side. "Martha?"

My mom looks at him and says, "No."

"Shit!" he says.

As soon as they're out of the house, I pick up the phone and dial Jane. "They're gone," I say.

We haul the boxes down from the attic.

"Are you sure you want to get rid of these?" Jane asks, holding up one of the paperbacks.

"You want them?" I say. "You can have them."

She pockets one or two.

I pull out my father's Zippo lighter and pick up one of the paperbacks and set fire to it and the box full of Polaroid photos.

Jane grabs the garden hose in case the flames get out of control.

MID-JULY, SOMEWHERE IN OKLAHOMA:

She's got a bruise under her right eye and a cut lip.

Sitting at the diner counter, I can't help but wonder where her abusive boyfriend is. And, right on cue, he comes back from the restroom and slides into the same side of the booth that she's sitting on. It's as if he thinks she's going to run off so he uses his body as a roadblock of sorts.

I touch Jane on the arm and nod my head in the couple's direction. Jane looks over at them and says, "What do you want to do about it?"

I think about it while we dig into burgers and down bottles of Coke. About midway through the meal, the boyfriend stands up and grabs the woman by the wrist. He pulls her from the booth behind him. I place my half-eaten burger back on the plate, toss some money on the counter. Jane follows close behind.

Outside, I yell over to the girl, "You can leave him anytime you like, you know."

She's timid as hell. She gets into the car and shuts the door behind her.

The boyfriend isn't so timid. He turns around and tells me to fuck myself.

I can't stop from laughing. Jane walks beside me and asks me again, "What do you want to do about it?"

I don't have to say a word. Jane knows. And we bum-rush the asshole. We beat him down. We punch him in the face. We knee him in the groin.

The girl gets out of the car. She screams for us to stop but we don't listen. She's not going to do anything to help herself. We pick up the boyfriend, and Jane fishes the keys out of his pocket. We toss him into the trunk of the car.

"Get in the car," I tell the girl. When she hesitates, I scream it at her. She obeys.

"Jane," I say, "follow us in the car, okay?"

We pull out of the diner's parking lot.

HALLOWEEN:

I always loved Halloween as a kid. A chance to play dress-up and get candy.

This year, I'm a waitress named Betty. Jane is going as Little Red Riding Hood. She looks so tasty, I'd love to be her Big Bad Wolf.

Delores says she hates Halloween. She says she's going to stay back at the motel tonight.

Killjoy.

Jane and I have found a party in Northern Texas (like it's hard to find a party on Halloween), and we're attending even if we weren't invited.

Something's in the punch. Jane says she's sick.

I want to stay at the party. I tell Jane to take the car, I'll find a way back.

When I do come back, I cannot believe what I see—Jane's head down between Delores' thighs.

I don't interrupt. I watch for only a moment.

Outside the door, I cry for the first time in a long time.

AUGUST:

Delores says that we need some cash if we're going to stay ahead of the law.

Staying ahead of the law means breaking the law, which means bringing even more heat.

It's a vicious circle.

We go further out of our comfort zone to get the cash.

We go to Kansas and knock over a bank.

"Money in the bag! No one moves, no one gets hurt!"

The tellers, all three of them, do what they're supposed to do when Jane gets to each of them: fill the bag with what's in their drawers and nothing more.

The aged guard is smart, too, not reaching for his gun and playing hero. I marvel at the restraint that these people have. If I were in their position,

I doubt that I'd be able to keep myself from going for my gun or trying to play hero, especially when I know that I'm being robbed by three women.

When we break out of the place and hop into the car, it's Delores that lets out the first war whoop. And then she gets to counting the cash as Jane peals us out of there.

After we've cleared town, Delores lets us in on the take.

"Seven thousand and fifty-two dollars," she says.

"We're rich!" Jane yells.

When we stop for the night, just beyond the Oklahoma border, I peroxide my hair.

Jane says, "I always wondered what you'd look like as a blonde. I like it." She kisses me. Delores is looking out the window, through the Venetian blinds, like she's expecting the other shoe to drop any moment.

MID-JULY, SOMEWHERE IN OKLAHOMA:

"He beats you and you keep taking it and you don't have to do that," I tell the girl. "Jane and I, we're gonna show you that you don't have to take it from that asshole."

We pull off on a county road in the middle of nowhere with nothing but fields and fields of corn.

Somewhere down the road, somewhere that feels right, I stop the car, and Jane pulls behind me a moment later.

I open the trunk and bring the asshole out, throwing him down in the dirt face-first. I kick him in the ribs, and then reach into the trunk and grab a tire iron. Jane opens our trunk and gets a tire iron out too.

The asshole gets up but we put him right back down with shots to the kneecaps.

We drag him into the cornfield and, when we're far enough in, I tell the girl to take the tire iron from me.

"Now," I say, "aim for his nose."

She has tears in her eyes. She's white-knuckling the tire iron.

"Do it," I say.

"Do it," Jane says.

Afterward, down the highway, the girl says, "My name's Delores."

EARLY-JULY:

We take the guy out to the shack that we've been going to ever since we became lovers.

We want his money. I want something else.

He's in his forties, wears a tie. He looks like an office worker. He even looks a little bit like him.

We lead him on back at the bar, making him think that he's going to get lucky tonight.

He asks if we do any kinky stuff, stuff with each other.

Jane smiles at me and says, "Oh, yeah."

I tell him that the shack is the best place for us; no one will bother us there.

He wheezes when I place the gun to his head. "I have a wife and kid," he says, begging me not to shoot him.

"Then you really shouldn't be here, should you?" I say.

It's when he tries to fight that I have no choice but to squeeze the trigger. His blood is hot on my face.

Jane grabs him by the ankles. "Get what's left of the head," she says. "Do you at least have a shovel in the trunk?"

NOVEMBER, BACK IN TEXAS:

Jane looks up at me from the floor. Delores is in the corner, trying to hold her guts in.

When she came in, Jane was smart enough to know what was going to happen. I think she even knew why.

Delores had no idea, and I didn't bother telling her. I just shot her in the stomach. Twice.

Jane tried to tackle me before I could turn the gun on her. And she kind of, sort of did. We wrestled for a while before I punched her in the face with the butt of the pistol.

Jane was always smart.

Outside, the jig is up. The cops are here.

"I loved you, baby," I tell Jane. For the first time that I can remember, I see fear in Jane's eyes. I pull back the hammer and fire one shot.

The noise dies down.

It starts up a moment later.

And then all is silent.

RED HOT
THOMAS PLUCK

Karen whipped down the bandana, and Bobby dropped the hammer. The shark-finned Studebaker roared away while the kid's silver blue Corvette spun its wheels and blew smoke. The Stude chirped through all four gears, leaving the rich kid two-car-lengths behind.

Bobby's heart swelled as he circled back to the line and saw Karen smiling. He had the fastest car on the track and the best girl. Karen had fiery Rita Hayworth curls and long legs to match. And now he had a new car to work on, the dumb kid's '58 Corvette.

The racing wasn't the kick. For Bobby, the kick was making that engine sing. Anyone could tear the fenders off a '32 five window coupe, put in a big mill, and be king of the quarter mile. Bobby liked to take a ride and turn it into a stone cold sleeper that looked bone stock but could blow away a wild gearhead's hot rod.

Karen smiled and patted the Stude's roof. When she didn't smile, she looked like she was squinting at something better up the road.

Bobby liked to keep her smiling.

She'd smiled at the silver blue Corvette when the freckle-faced kid cruised in. The boy had strutted up in his varsity jacket and asked if she wanted a ride.

"You're talking to my wife, kid."

"Who you calling kid, little man?"

Small but rawboned, Bobby smirked. "You got balls, kid. But does your ride?"

So they raced for pink slips. If Bobby lost, Karen went for a ride with the kid in his Corvette.

Now the kid's cornfed friends made noise about a hustle, while bikers took over the drag strip. One kid rattled a tire chain. Bobby hadn't rumbled in a dog's age, but these kids looked soft. The other hot rodders watched, and Bobby knew a few would back him up if it came to that.

"Let's go," Karen said. "They're a bunch of bullies."

Bobby stared across the lot at the teenagers working each other up for a fight.

"Don't let 'em make you jealous, Daddy," Karen said and kissed his forehead.

Bobby nodded and slid a wrench into his pocket, just in case. He kept his eyes on the kids as he crossed the blacktop.

"You can keep the 'Vette," Bobby said. "It ain't got any balls anyway."

"You're a cheater," the kid hollered. "She signaled you early."

"You want a rematch?"

The kid grabbed his collar. "I want my ride with your wife, shorty."

Bobby closed his fist around the wrench as the kid steamed up his face. Then the kid levitated, eyes gone wide.

A beefy man in a motorcycle jacket had the teen by the scruff. "I don't like you picking on my little brother," the man said. "What's the problem here?"

"Kid here lost his pink slip," Bobby said loud, for the crowd. "Now he's welching."

"She signaled him early," Freckles said.

"No one likes a welcher, kid," the biker said.

The teenager with the chain snapped it against the biker's leather jacket. The biker looped his arm under it, yanked the big kid holding it toward him, and stopped his momentum with a head butt to the nose.

The other teens took a step with their tire irons, and the biker produced a well-worn Randall knife, pointing at each belly in turn. "You all want to kiss your mommies goodnight tonight, doncha? Then beat it. And don't bother the grown-ups."

The bloody-nosed kid cupped his face and stumbled away. His friends pushed him in the back of a wagon. Freckles climbed into his Corvette and hollered, "You know who my old man is? You're in big trouble," before peeling away.

Bobby slapped the biker's arm and shook his hand. "Thanks, Troy."

"Figured I oughtta see how little brother made a name for himself," Troy said, sliding the knife into his engineer's boot. "I was gonna see if you learned to scrap, but hey, old habits die hard."

"I can hold my own these days."

"Didn't look like it," Troy smiled. "You got a woman like that, men are gonna look at her. I'll be in town a while, if you need a bodyguard again."

Karen smiled. "Bobby told me about you," she said and offered her hand. "You were like brothers."

"We are brothers," Bobby said. "Troy, this is Karen. My wife."

"And a beautiful wife she is," Troy said, holding her hand a little too long.

• • •

Troy followed them on his motorcycle out on the highway, and they caught up over quarts of beer, cheeseburgers and fried clam strips at a road-stand called The Three Acre Grill. Troy told them that after the war, he picked up a surplus Scout in California and rode it up the coast. He tapped two medals pinned to his jacket, a dead German's Iron Cross and a Purple Heart.

"Your Indian sounds like she's losing compression," Bobby said. "Bring her to the shop, I'll fix her up."

"I dunno," Troy said. "I been riding alone a long time. It's time I got something with two seats instead of one. I can still turn a wrench, if you need a second man."

Bobby chewed on a clam strip and laughed to himself. "I should know better, but it's good to have you back, brother."

They offered Troy the sofa, but he said he had a bed at a boarding house, and the old lady made good breakfast.

• • •

That night, after they made love, Karen rested her head on Bobby's chest and asked about Troy.

"His Dad was my father's mechanic," Bobby said. "He could tune valves like nobody's business. Had a magic ear. He and his wife got creamed by a coal truck driver who fell asleep at the wheel. Troy was in back."

Bobby stroked her hair while he talked. "Mine took him in because he was like the big brother I never had. I did his homework, and he had my back in the schoolyard. He's a good guy, but he never knows what's good for him."

"What do you mean?"

"My father said he'd buy Troy a car, if he went to prep school and stopped fooling around," Bobby said. "It wasn't much, a Model A Ford with a rumble seat. But we made that baby sing. We had a lot of fun, until the Japs hit Pearl."

Bobby didn't tell her that without him to do his homework, Troy flunked out. His father demanded the car back. Troy called it his inheritance, and his old man, an accountant, pulled out a ledger showing every expense he'd paid in raising him.

They had a big fight, and Troy ran away with the Ford. When his father reported it stolen, Troy parked it over a leaf pile and let it burn, rather than give it back.

Bobby stared at the ceiling, recalling the flames.

Karen kissed down his chest, and Bobby stayed her with his hand. "I'm tuckered out, baby. Come up here." She crawled up with a pout, curled up with her head on his chest and his thumb in her mouth to fall asleep.

Bobby met her after the war, when he'd used GI bill money to open the shop and build his first rod, a flathead Ford someone had plowed into a guardrail. He unbent the frame, hopped-up the engine, and drove it to every drag strip he could find. On the afternoon he took five C-notes off a moonshiner in the Pines, he saw a dusty girl thumbing it barefoot on a country road.

"Where you headed?"

"Wherever you're going, Daddy. Nice wheels."

She put her head in his lap when they hit the highway. He pulled her back up. "What, are you queer?" she asked.

"No, and I keep my money in my boot. You're welcome to it, if that's what you want."

"I wasn't gonna rob you," she said. "I just need a ride out of here. I didn't want you dumping me in the sticks. The last bastard kicked me out and kept my shoes."

"You hungry?"

He took her home and made potted meat sandwiches while she scrubbed herself down. They ate them with cans of Rheingold beer and danced round the radio to Alan Freed's *Moondog Hour*. She danced him right into the bedroom and stayed the weekend. Monday morning, she was still there, and the next. He taught her to spin a wrench. She liked to work hard all week and play in bed all weekend. That suited him just fine.

Six years, and some nights she still woke up crying. The thumb helped. Her people had hurt her bad, and he'd tried to wean her off the strange quirks that came with that, but instead, they'd cozied up to his own. Guys poked fun, Little Bobby Cee and his treetop redheaded girl. They didn't laugh when Bobby drove away with their money in his pocket and his arm around her, his foot on the gas and her hand working the stick, like a finely tuned machine.

"Goodnight baby," he whispered.

"Mm-hmm," she said. He fell asleep smelling her hair, Ivory Soap and exhaust.

...

In the morning, they installed a six pack of Weber carbs on a Model T hot rod while finishing off drop biscuits and a pot of black coffee. Troy hadn't shown by noon when a thin man in a suit pulled up in the silver blue Corvette with a fat man in a Lincoln trailing behind. They walked into the shop without asking, their loafers dodging oil stains. Wrinkled their noses at the radio blaring rockabilly.

"Mr. Cohn, we're here to discuss a sale," Skinny said.

Bobby tucked his shop rag in his back pocket. "I don't have any cars for sale at the moment."

"It's a trade," Fatty said, removing a money clip from his pocket. "The Corvette for the Studebaker."

"She's not for sale."

"My son says he wants it." The Fat Man smiled and began peeling off hundred dollar bills. "Say when."

The new bills rasped against each other. Bobby turned back to his work. When Fatty got to four, Karen inhaled. She squeezed Bobby's arm.

At six, Bobby turned. "You still there?"

"You people are something," the Fat Man said. "I'm paying double, and I get guff."

"My Stude's twice the car your bigmouth son's is."

The Fat Man peeled a seventh, and Bobby nodded.

He flicked the bills at Bobby's chest and waddled back to the Lincoln. "Exchange the titles," he said to Skinny. "I'm done with this trash."

Bobby stared at the man's back as the greenbacks fluttered in the breeze. The Stude had been a rich man's car. After he'd blown the engine, Bobby bought it cheap. *Easy come, easy go.* Karen snatched up the bills, while he traded pinks with the man's lackey.

"Mr. Muntz is something else, isn't he?" Skinny mumbled under his breath.

Bobby said nothing and tucked the Corvette's title into his pocket. He squinted as the Studebaker disappeared up the road.

Karen clapped her hands and smiled. "Daddy, you sure spoil me rotten," she said. "Ready for lunch?"

"Not hungry yet."

She tugged the belt loops of his jeans. "Then let's work up an appetite."

...

Bobby ate a potted meat sandwich and thought about the Corvette while Karen showered off the sex and engine grease. He'd never worked with fuel injection before. And convertibles were heavy. It would be a challenge to make it work, and that's where he got his kicks.

Karen toweled dry in the kitchen and danced around him, red curls tumbling down. "You've got that car on the brain already," she said and rubbed her hip against his shoulder. "Don't forget me."

He gave her rear end a pat.

"You call that a love tap," she purred. "Fill up my tummy."

"Tonight, baby," he said, and kissed her belly. "We got to finish that Merc."

She pouted. "Promise."

"Cross my heart."

She ruffled his hair and smiled.

"Go put some clothes on."

She tiptoed into the bedroom, towel trailing on the floor.

Bobby watched her go. She'd grown up hard and was all mixed up when he found her. Knelt when she wanted things. And if she didn't get it, she'd try to taunt him into using his hands.

"I'm not going to hit you," he'd told her, the first time.

She slapped him across the face. It stung, like nostalgia.

"I'm not gonna hate you, either."

"But I'm bad," she'd said. Eyes red. Lip quivering.

"No you're not," he said. "To me, you're gold."

He found a washer in his pocket and slipped it on her ring finger. She gripped fistfuls of his hair and kissed him, hard. Bobby sold his flathead Ford to swap the washer on her finger for a wedding band.

...

Troy puttered his bike to a stop beside the big, black Mercury. Bobby stood on the bumper, watching Karen adjust the points. She'd changed back into cut-off jeans and a tied-off work shirt.

"That's perfect, baby."

Troy swung his leg off the cycle and leaned it against the garage.

"Hi Troy," Karen said.

"We like to start before noon," Bobby said.

Troy smiled. "I like the night shift."

"We're a nine to five shop."

"All right," Troy said. "No wonder you got your wife working. You scared the last guy off."

"I like fixing them," Karen said. "I'm getting pretty good."

"I'm sure you are, honey." Troy hung his leather jacket on the handlebars of his bike. "What's the Merc getting?"

"Valve job," Bobby said.

"My specialty. Fire her up."

The valves rattled like a wind chime. Troy took a screwdriver and held the point against the valve covers, his ear against it like a stethoscope. Karen watched with hands on her hips.

"Three, six and eight," Troy said.

They torqued off the covers, and Troy adjusted the valves with the finesse of a piano tuner. He slapped a cover back on and twisted the first nut.

"Aren't you going to check first?" Karen asked.

"Bet you a cold one she runs smooth as a baby's ass."

"He's a natural," Bobby said. "Just like his old man."

Troy tightened the rest and winked at Karen. "Fire her up, Red."

Karen smirked and twisted the key. The Merc purred.

Troy showed off a chipped front tooth. "How about that cold beer you owe me, Red?"

"My name's Karen," she said. "You call me Red and I'm calling you Bluto."

Troy scratched his beard and watched her head inside. "What happened to the Studebaker?"

Bobby told him.

"I wouldn't've given that pig the satisfaction," Troy said. "Don't you got self-respect?"

"Yeah," Bobby said and shrugged. "I got bills to pay, too. Plus, Karen liked it."

"And baby gets what baby wants," Troy said.

Karen came back with three beers. She peeled the top off one and slugged it back, wiping the foam off her lips with a catlike grin.

"I don't blame you," Troy said.

...

After they closed shop, Karen and Bobby took the Corvette out to the highway. She smiled ear to ear, bare feet on the pedals and Bobby's hand on her thigh, squeezing to signal her when to power shift.

"I don't like the bucket seats," she hollered. "You're so far away."

Troy buzzed in their wake on the Indian. Bobby looked back.

"C'mon baby," he said. "Lose him."

Her painted toes pushed the pedal down and Troy vanished into a black dot. They pulled over at Rutt's Hut, a brick shack that sold fried hot dogs and served as the local cruise spot. A few rodders already held court, and they pointed at the lady driver as she pumped the clutch and let the engine roar, rolling into a spot.

Karen kissed Bobby with a wicked grin, silencing the hoots and whistles from the greaser crowd.

When Troy caught up, they ordered a box of hot dogs and ate sitting on the guard rail, listening to the radio and watching other cruisers roll in.

"The kid stripped the rear gears," Bobby said. "I'm gonna put in a Studebaker rear tomorrow. Limited slip."

"You're tearing her apart already," Karen said and pouted.

"You can ride my bike until he's done," Troy said, licking his fingers.

"I've never rode a motorcycle before," she said.

"I'll show ya. It's like, well, riding a bike."

Karen turned to Bobby. "Can I?"

"I dunno," Bobby said. "It's dangerous."

"C'mon, brother." Troy smiled, dimpling his stubbled cheeks. "Think I'd let some broad crash my bike?"

"OK," Bobby said. "Just be careful."

Karen smiled and kissed Bobby on the cheek.

Older models rolled in. The country had slumped, and the men who hadn't been laid off clutched their purse strings. The Corvette caught a lot of eyes, and Bobby made the rounds, letting his skill on flatheads and late model mills be known.

Karen sat on the Corvette's back bumper, and Troy made to sit next to her.

"Take your jacket off," she said. "I don't want them buckles scratching my paint."

Troy smirked and shrugged it off, baring a tight white tee shirt.

"Your paint, huh? You got him wrapped around your finger, don't you? How'd the squirt get his hands on a bombshell like you?"

"He gave me a lift when I needed one."

Troy fished the Luckies out of his pocket, tapped one out, offered it to her.

"No thanks."

"I'd hate for 'em to stunt your growth," Troy said, then lit up. He puffed and watched the crowd. Traded hairy eyeballs with a motor cop.

Karen stuck her face in the smoke, inhaled. "Mmm," she said. "I used to smoke, before Bobby."

"He make you stop?"

"No, I just stopped. He don't, so I don't."

"Don't tell me you don't want one."

Her wide grin curled at one end, and her cheeks flushed.

Troy held out the cigarette, and she leaned to take a long puff.

"Mmm, never smoked a tailor made before," she said.

"What else does he tell you not to do?"

...

Bobby found the brothers who bought his Ford coupe and admired what they'd done to it. As testament to its sleeper nature, they'd hand painted little black Z's along the chrome but otherwise kept it clean. It stood out among the garish, flamed-out rods and lead barges that couldn't get out of their own way. Bobby shook the Puerto Rican boys' hands. Told them he had some new tricks and to stop by the shop when they had green to spend.

He wandered back toward the car, knowing it would never be a sleeper but it could be a champ. Bumped into someone handing out flyers advertising a race sponsored by the National Hot Rod Association. Bobby took one and found Karen laughing with Troy.

"There's a big race at the track in Moonachie next month, Karen," Bobby said. "Your 'Vette's gonna win it."

...

Karen took her first motorcycle lesson the next morning. She traded her clogs for a pair of Bobby's boots and rode out clutching Troy's barrel chest. She smiled back to Bobby as they took off.

Bobby watched them vanish around a curve and swapped the Corvette's gears to get his mind off it.

Troy arrived earlier each day, teaching Karen to ride the bike when it was slow, working under a hood when it was busy. The Corvette's new gears made the tires break loose easy, so Bobby ordered a pair of Traction Master bars from the parts shop.

"I'm scared to drive her now," Karen said. "She's all over the place."

"You got to feather the clutch until I get the traction bars on," Bobby said from beneath a Chrysler with a leaky transmission. "I'll show you later."

"I'll show her," Troy said. "We'll bring back lunch."

"Don't smoke the tires too much," Bobby called. "They're barely broken in."

Troy said, "I'll treat her like a virgin."

• • •

Bobby thought about the Corvette while he worked on the Chrysler. He could drop a Hemi in it. It would steer like a boat, but would fly with the right traction bars. Ugly, but effective. That wasn't his way. It had to be perfect.

A familiar exhaust note broke his train of thought.

He rolled out on the creeper. His old Studebaker Hawk revved at the curb. Freckles sneered from the driver's seat and stepped out with three friends. The one Troy clocked had his nose bandaged and two black eyes.

"I told your Pop the sale was final, kid."

"My old man said you Jewed him for this piece of shit," Freckles said. "It don't even got air conditioning."

"It's all about speed, kid." Bobby stood up and plucked a breaker bar off the bench, holding it alongside his leg.

"Stop calling him kid, Christkiller," Broken Nose honked. "It's too bad the Krauts didn't get all of you."

"Gonna tell you once," Bobby said. "Get off my property."

They laughed and kicked loose parts around.

"My father could buy you," Freckles said. "You know who he is? He owns the Chevy dealership. His mechanic's figuring out your tricks. We're gonna wipe you off the map so you can't rip people off no more."

Freckles hawked up a wad and spat it on the concrete.

"Everybody knows you cheated now," he sneered. "I got your wheels to prove it."

Bobby looked at the phone. The cops wouldn't even show up. The town welcomed his speed shop as they would a pool hall or a bucket of blood tavern that served Negroes alongside whites.

The boys filled the garage door, their shadows darkening the workshop.

"Where's that hot wife of yours, Jewboy?" Freckles said, knocking parts off the shelves.

Bobby swung, and the kid skipped back.

"How'd she wind up with a sawed-off kike, like you?"

Bobby lashed again, clanging the bar off a shelf, sending coffee cans of nuts and washers pattering to the floor. "Get the hell out of here!"

"Crazy Jew bastard!" The kids yelled and scattered.

Bobby chased them to the street.

"You going to the big race, oven dodger? We'll be there! We're gonna kick your ass!"

Freckles popped the clutch and sent the black-finned Hawk fishtailing up the road. He threw the bar after them, and it rang off the pavement, clattering to the curb. The car shrank in the distance, like a fist around his heart. Bobby walked back to the garage and bent down to clean up the scattered parts.

...

His stomach grumbled by the time Troy and Karen came back in the Corvette, smelling of sweat and cigarettes. Troy tossed him a sack of burgers, and Karen ran inside, coming out with a six pack of Rheingold.

"Where'd you go?" Bobby said, biting into a cold burger.

"I had to take her out on the highway to get a handle on it," Troy said, wiping mustard on his sleeve. "So we stopped at the Red Chimney."

"Sorry they're cold," Karen said. "I want a shower. It was hot with the top down."

"Don't you want to eat with us?"

"I'm not that hungry," she said. "I'll warm mine up in the oven."

"OK," Bobby said, and she scampered inside.

"She's something else," Troy said.

"That she is," Bobby said, ticking off parts in his head. He needed someone who knew fuel injection. Hotter plugs and wires to handle the fuel, fatter pipes to handle the exhaust. One thing led to another. Might as well give it the whole schmear and win back his Stude from that Kraut son of a bitch.

...

That night, Karen slipped into the claw foot tub while Bobby showered, his head full of engines. He felt her nipples harden against his shoulder blades, and she kneaded his temples under the hot water.

"You're thinking too hard, Daddy," she said. "Grinding your teeth."

He turned, and she cradled his head against her breasts. He let her crush the bad thoughts out of his head. Thoughts about the Freckles kid and about Troy.

When Troy went off to war, he'd left a girl pregnant. Roxy Turner.

When she started showing, she lost her carhop job at Stewart's. Bobby helped her take care of it and kept her company until the Army stretched its measuring tape and put him to work in the motor pool.

Bobby felt himself hardening between Karen's thighs.

She reached down and held him. "You gonna fill my tummy now?"

Bobby sighed into her chest. When they first met, her compulsion had been exciting, especially on long drives. It made him feel like a bigger man, instead of a mustached kid married to a statuesque knockout. After a while, it began to feel like ritual, salting a wound deep inside her, one that would never heal.

She raked her short nails down his chest as she made to slide down. He caught her and kissed her on the mouth. Tasted the tobacco.

"You smoking again?"

"Just a couple," she said. "Now and then."

"I don't like when you smoke," he said. "It tastes like a tailpipe."

She frowned and stepped out of the shower, slipping on the tile. She caught herself and yanked a towel off the bar before stomping out.

"Karen," he called after her and sighed.

After he dried off, he found her curled on the bed, wrapped in a towel. He spooned behind her, nuzzling the fine hairs on the very back of her neck.

"I'm sorry, baby."

"You said I taste like garbage."

"No, you don't. You taste sweeter than peaches right out of the can," he said, kissing her freckled shoulder.

"You should dump me back where you found me," she said.

"Where would I be without my fire cat?"

"I can't give you no son," she shuddered. "What am I good for?"

"You're a pretty damn good mechanic."

She reached up and clutched his hand.

Bobby squeezed the sobs out of her, rocking side to side.

...

In the morning, Bobby bolted the tractions bars on the Corvette while Karen worked on a Packard's carburetor. Bobby made a few calls, tracking down a mechanic he knew from the service. Lenny Fetter had worked on B-29's and had brought home a sweet Alfa Romeo from Italy, tricked out with electronic fuel injection. Now he worked for Bendix, which liked to keep cozy with the Air Force.

Karen pointed up the road and Bobby saw Troy pushing his bike toward the shop. Bobby hung up the phone as Troy pushed the bike into the garage.

"She finally quit me," Troy said.

"You should've took better care of her."

"I got you to fix my mistakes," Troy said. "Can I get a cold beer, Red? I walked it from the river."

"She's working on something," Bobby said, but Karen put down her tools and went in.

"You heard about Roxy, huh?"

"She wrote some nasty letters," Troy said.

Karen came back with three cans of beer.

"Thanks, baby, but I got to meet an old buddy from the service, about the 'Vette," Bobby said. "You two eat without me, but don't work on the bike until the Packard's done."

"Yessir," Troy barked and snapped a salute.

Karen laughed.

"I served too, you know," Bobby said, walking to the green flareside pick-up truck.

"Yeah, rear echelon." Troy tossed back his beer.

"Someone had to keep the tanks rolling," Bobby said, climbing into the truck.

...

Bobby met Lenny at the Bendix diner car, a silver capsule planted on a triangle in the middle of Route 17. The red Alfa sat low, all sweeping curves, like a crimson wave about to break. They squeezed into a booth and talked injectors, jets and spark over club sandwiches. The Rochester unit that Chevrolet used in the Corvette was touchy, Lenny said. The Alfa Romeo had an electronic unit, which was pricey and hard to find.

Bobby slipped Len one of the Fat Man's hundred dollar bills to get the spare fuel injection system he kept in his garage and to let him drive the Italian roadster to get it.

"That's what I don't understand with you hot rodders," Len shouted over the wind, as they flew down the road. "By the time you're done hopping up some jalopy, you could get one that's showroom new."

"It's not about money," Bobby said. "It's about making it your own."

Lenny had a garage full of parts for the roadster. He picked out three boxes labeled in Italian and a dog-eared manual. "Here you go."

"One more thing for my C-note," Bobby said. "You still got contacts in the service, I hear."

"There's rumor to that effect," Lenny said, cupping his hand to whisper. "Something I need to know."

...

When Bobby got back, the Packard was done, and they had the bike's engine apart on a blanket, picking over pieces like a game of checkers.

"I figured out what's wrong with the bike," Karen said. "We need some parts, though."

He walked over, stroked her hair. "Smart as she is beautiful."

Troy smiled. "She's pretty smart for a split tail."

Karen blushed.

"I gotta untangle this injector setup," Bobby said. "The 'Vette's gonna be out of commission a while. Take the Ford."

They climbed into the pickup truck and headed out.

...

Bobby lost himself in the challenge. The Corvette flooded, even with hot plugs. The manual was written in Italian. Other than a few exploded diagrams, it was only good for throwing across the garage. When Karen and Troy returned, he waved at them and went back to work.

"I'm gonna take a shower," Karen called. "That truck's so hot."

"OK baby," he said, not turning around.

Troy removed his jacket, then peered over the work bench. "You got a 9/16ths Crescent wrench?"

"Yeah," Bobby said, twisting a ratchet.

"Where?"

"On the damn bench!"

"Whoa, what's eating you?"

"Nothing." He disconnected the last bolt and started over, frowning at the grease-stained manual.

"You want a hand?"

"I got it."

Troy dug around on the bench, picking up one wrench, dropping it, picking up another. "You sure you don't got the 9/16ths in your pocket?"

"I got the 5/8ths," Bobby said. "I just need five minutes of unbroken concentration, all right?"

"All right, but don't give me attitude."

Bobby glared. "Quit busting my balls!"

Troy froze, lip curled in a grin. He plucked a wrench from the pile and walked to the motorcycle.

Bobby saw Karen standing at the front door, chewing gum with her hair turbaned in a towel.

"Everything OK?" she said.

"Just little Bobby's temper," Troy said. "Always got him in trouble."

"Lay off, Troy," Bobby said. "I'm not in the mood."

"It's okay," Karen said. "It's how he gets when he's working hard on something."

"You two should try it sometime," Bobby said. "Working hard. You been gallivanting around all damn week."

"You're all worked up," Karen said, kissing him quick. Tasting of smoke and licorice. "You need me?"

Bobby gripped the fender. "I just need some peace and quiet to figure this out."

"Then I'm gonna start dinner," she said.

"Fine," Bobby said and went back under the hood as she walked inside.

"You shouldn't talk to her like that," Troy said.

"Mind your own business."

Bobby twisted the key, and the Corvette bucked and stalled from starvation. He took it apart and started again. By the time they lost the daylight, Troy had the bike together and headed inside to say goodbye to Karen. When he left, Bobby hung a light under the hood and cursed to himself, studying the manual's tiny illustrations.

Karen came up behind him, slipping her arms around his waist.

"You cool off yet?"

"Just another minute, baby."

She held him as the minute stretched to ten, and his sighs rose louder. She walked back inside and ate dinner alone. She watched his plate get cold and read a paperback of *Peyton Place* until her head started dipping into the book. She crawled into bed to wait for him, but fell asleep before he joined her.

When Karen woke to the sound of the engine revving, she threw a robe around herself and walked outside barefoot. Up the street, light bulbs popped on in second-floor windows.

"Bobby," she called into the open garage. She found him sneering behind the wheel of the Corvette, revving the engine.

"I did it, Karen. Listen to her," he hollered.

"Come inside, baby. It's late," she said, leaning her elbows on the door.

He killed the engine and reached up to unknot her hair, spilling it down. She kneaded the back of his neck, and he spread her robe open, nuzzling inside.

"Your mustache tickles," she said, laughing. "Let's go inside."

"I thought you liked it in the car," he said, unbuckling his jeans.

"It's cold out here," she said, reaching down and warming him. She ran inside, holding her robe closed with one hand, tugging him along with the other.

They made it as far as the kitchen. She shucked the robe and sank to her knees, cream skin glowing in the dim light. A purple bruise marked her behind, but Bobby was too distracted to ask about it, and she was in no position to answer.

He ran his hands through her hair and met her eyes, the way she liked. She asked for a lot of things he wouldn't do. He'd tried, but didn't like how he felt while doing it, or how she reacted. This, well, he wouldn't say he didn't enjoy it, or reciprocating.

But it all came back to that first ride, when he'd picked her up, and she fell into it like she'd been raised on it. He shuddered at the thought.

Karen mistook his shiver for another involuntary reaction and murmured in anticipation. That set him off, and she gripped his thighs as he hunched over and didn't stop until he begged.

He carried her to bed, completing the ritual. Tucking her in, spooning up behind her, rocking.

He ran his fingers up her thigh, to please her in return.

"Don't ruin it," she said.

"What am I going to ruin? You got what you wanted," he said. "What about what I want?"

"I gave you what all men want," she said, tiredly.

"I want to make you happy, baby."

"I am happy, Daddy."

"You know what I mean."

"You want me? Go ahead." She lifted one knee, offering herself.

"Damn it, Karen. What's wrong, baby? You haven't acted like this since forever."

"Use me," she said. "I know you want to. I feel you back there."

"My back hurts, baby. Let me put you to sleep."

"I'm not even good for that anymore," she said, flat.

"Karen," he sighed and knelt to see her face. Bruises marred her behind. "How'd you get these?"

"I fell off the bike," she said.

He traced the bruise with his fingers. Like the ones she'd had when he first found her. Only bigger this time, from larger hands.

Bobby's heart dropped from his chest, leaving a cold, empty space the wind could rattle through.

"Damn it, Karen. Why?"

"I don't know," she said. "It just happened."

"What does that even mean? Don't I give you everything? For that, you break my heart?"

"Not everything," she said, "I'm bad. I need someone to keep me in line." She writhed, her hands sweeping slow over her body.

"I told you, baby. You're gold."

"I don't deserve you," she said. "You know it. I see it in your eyes, when other men look at me. How you puff up, ready to fight. 'Cause I'm a little whore who gets them all worked up," she said, running a finger up her thigh.

"Don't talk like that."

"Troy doesn't give me no thumb," she husked. "No sir, he pushes me right down on it and smacks me hard. He knows what I deserve."

Bobby raised his hand, trembling with rage.

"C'mon, hit me! Act like a man!" Karen braced and closed her eyes.

Bobby's hand fluttered above his shoulder, fell to his side.

Karen deflated slow, her head lolling, hair spilling over her chest. She opened her eyes, saw Bobby staring at his hand. She covered herself. "I'm sorry, Bobby," she said. "You can't fix me."

She curled into a ball and put her thumb in her own mouth.

Bobby fell asleep staring at her shoulders.

· · ·

In the morning, Bobby pulled the sheets to her chin and took the Corvette out for a run. Counting off the telephone poles as he roared down Highway 21, he knew the car was his fastest. Cold comfort against the fire in his brain.

He stopped at a diner over the bridge and ordered eggs on toast.

"Adam and Eve on a raft," the waitress called into the kitchen. "You want those scrambled, honey?"

Bobby blinked, nodded.

"Wreck 'em," she hollered.

He poked at the eggs with his fork, bloodied them with ketchup, and forced them down to fill the pit in his gut.

...

Bobby nosed the Corvette along the river's snaky curves until he reached the big houses and tall trees of his old neighborhood. He knew this side of the river. The brick castle of the high school with boys and girls lining up at separate doors. The baseball diamond where Troy had fought for him, the runt who they always picked last. The service station Troy's Pop had run. The cul-de-sac Bobby grew up on.

He parked in a bulldozed lot alongside the water and killed the engine.

The night Troy stormed out, Bobby told his old man he was wrong, to let his brother keep the car so he could go make his own way.

"He's not your brother, Robert," his father said. "He's not blood. He's the help. You needed a friend, and you couldn't make any. Do you understand? He's the son of a grease monkey, not like you. Why do you think he needs you to do his homework?" He removed his half-moon eyeglasses. "You think he'd be your friend if his father hadn't worked for me?"

Thanks to the stubbornness of youth and the loyalty of the schoolyard, Bobby said some ugly things right back. He spent the night on the porch while his mother pleaded his case. Her argument ended with a slap, a muffled wail, and running up the steps to the bedroom.

Bobby stood at the door with fists at his sides, killing his old man a thousand times in his head. When the lock clicked shut, he started walking to Troy and Roxy's flop across the tracks. He knocked hard on the door and heard lots of laughing and scrambling before Troy answered in his boxer shorts. Bobby slept on the floor, covering his ears against the mattress squeaking.

He played hooky the next day and drank with them. Roxy danced to the radio in her slip, pointing and laughing when she caught Bobby blushing and hiding an erection. That night, a Negro knocked on the door and said the police were sniffing around. Bobby fell asleep in a chair with a bottle of wine.

He woke to sirens and an empty room. Outside, he followed kids hollering about a fire. Down by the river, the Model A's flaming corpse lit up the water and the faces of poor folks who got out of bed to watch the firemen. Troy tried to piss on it and a policeman dragged him away.

The judge told him jail or the Marines. Troy picked Parris Island. The recruiter kicked Bobby out, and he chose Roxy's sofa over heading home. He pumped gas, and she wore a girdle and car hopped. Together they paid the bills.

She hid her tears for Troy, and Bobby hid tears for his mother. Roxy had gloss black hair and curves Bobby couldn't keep his eyes off of, pregnant or not. After work, they ate cans of chili and drank white port, listening to her shabby radio. Roxy taught him to dance, then how to kiss, and one night when she felt especially low, she taught him to make love.

Bobby felt like a man, bringing home his meager bucks from the Sinclair station to find her heating up dinner, rocking her hips to the bluegrass music of Don Larkin's *Hometown Frolics*, a bottle of wine in her hand. They'd smoke by the river, skip stones, and fool around. When they finished, she'd lock her ankles behind him and tell him to never let him go. He'd sneak out in the morning to scrub off the itch in the wash room down the hall.

When Roxy got bigger, the landlady said she couldn't stay on living there unless she saw Doctor Von Roth, down by the river. Bobby paid for the cab and held her hand for the ride. When Bobby told him the address, the cabbie said it would be an extra buck.

He took them to a red shingled house with a dozen cats watching from the porch. A Black Maria rusted in the weeds out back.

They found the doctor sleeping on a stained armchair, his liver spotted cheeks hanging beneath hollow eyes. He took Bobby's money and looped a thin arm around Roxy's hips, leading her in the back. Bobby found the cabby asleep, so he sat on the porch, scratching a crusty-eyed cat under the chin.

A half hour later a puffy-eyed Roxy hobbled out, gripping the doctor's shoulder. The doc shoved bottles into Bobby's hands, sulfa pills and codeine syrup, the instructions scrawled on a scrap of brown paper bag. Back in their room, Bobby eased her to the mattress and fed her the medicine with a spoon. He rubbed her shoulder until her crying stopped, then drank port until he could fall asleep and stop wondering if the doctor buried the babies or just tossed them into the river.

In the morning, he rubbed Roxy's shoulder and found it cold. He tore off the quilt, baring sheets slick and red. The codeine was gone, and so was she. Bobby gathered his things and found an Army recruiter who measured his height on tiptoes.

...

A motorcycle cop rapped his nightstick on the seat rest, and Bobby snapped out of it, looking up at the officer's square, clean-shaved face.

"You can't park here," he said.

"I was just leaving, sir." Bobby fired up the engine, goosing the pedal to keep it from stalling.

"Kind of loud," the officer said. "If you don't get that taken care of, I'll have to write a ticket."

"I'll fix it," he said and eased into gear. When the cop turned his bike around at the town line, Bobby dropped the hammer and hugged the river all the way home.

In the kitchen, he stared at the linoleum by the bedroom door, taking deep breaths. He thought of the best times. The first morning when she made him breakfast. The night she took his ring.

A ring she wore while fooling around with Troy, the little whore.

Bobby ground his teeth. They had to talk it out, and words could hurt more than a slap ever could. That he knew.

He settled on a memory of how proud he was, the first time she fixed a customer's car without any help. That smile. That was the Karen he married, the one he loved. They'd get past this. They'd be stronger than before, he told himself.

He opened the door to an empty bed.

...

Later, he sat on the bed with a Luger he'd bought off a tank gunner back from the front. He cycled all the rounds through the chamber, then reloaded. Like clockwork. You had to hand it to the Krauts. They could build a machine. He clicked the safety on and tucked it under his shirt.

Bobby found the phone book and called the boarding houses he knew. Nothing. Dialed the operator, had her connect him to ones he didn't know. They didn't have a resident with a motorcycle. They wouldn't allow one.

They wouldn't let him bring a woman home, either. *Stupid.* Then he'd check the motels on the highway. He walked to the door with purpose, and the phone rang as his hand touched the knob.

He took a big breath, put the receiver to his ear.

"Hello? Is this Bobby Cohn?"

"Yes."

"Hey, it's Lenny. How's that setup working for you?"

Bobby sighed and shook his head. "If you'd told me what a pain in the ass it was to install, I'd have paid you half. But it works. You find that other thing out for me?"

"Yeah, that's what I'm calling about. Troy Peterson, Marines. We got one who was KIA on Peleliu. Says he was born in Wisconsin, in 1917."

"This one's breathing," Bobby said.

"OK. The other one? Says he was born in Brooklyn, '24. Dishonorable discharge."

"He's got a purple heart. They let you keep those?"

"Check the back," Lenny said. "His name should be on it."

"But how would he get it?"

"Steal it. Or buy it."

"Who'd sell a medal?"

"Someone who came home hurting, Bobby. The VA won't give you morphine if you're on two feet. We get fellas applying for work here, they know we like veterans. So they buy one off a rummy."

"So give me the skinny."

"PFC Peterson spent the war in the brig. They released him in '47."

"What for?"

"He went AWOL in Pendleton," Lenny said. "Right before they shipped out. Busted an officer's jaw, stole his Plymouth. They caught him a couple of months later up the coast in San Bernardino, shacked up with a hooker."

"Well uh, thanks, Lenny. I knew he was full of shit, just not this bad."

"He's not the first to lie about it," Lenny said. "Everyone stormed the beach at Normandy, you know."

"Everybody but us," Bobby said and hung up.

...

Bobby searched motel parking lots for Troy's Indian until dark, even circling the Howard Johnson's. Where Troy would get that kind of scratch, he didn't know. A flop in Newark was more likely. Bobby knew a couple of Nicky Newarks, tough guys who hot rodded. One of them might know where bikers holed up. He headed for Rutt's Hut.

He rolled in behind a chopped '49 Merc lead sled and scanned for the Indian, Karen's red curls, or Troy's crooked smile. He came up empty and doubled back, eyeballing the cars for one he recognized, thumbing the band of gold on his finger to keep from making a fist.

At the far end of the lot, Freckles leaned on the Studebaker's fender, laughing it up with his friends.

Bobby gripped the Luger, blood rushing to his face. He'd never fired a pistol, but saw himself executing them. Little round holes in their foreheads, like the mounds of prisoners they found in the camps when the tanks rolled in.

He squeezed the Luger's checkered grips, tossed it in the seat next to him. He let the engine loose on the highway, hellish hot summer wind rushing past his face. It had felt like freedom, once.

What was love? He didn't know. He knew he and Karen were two busted parts that had worked together. She needed saving, and he'd needed to save someone.

He pulled into the driveway. The Indian leaned against the garage. He ran inside.

"Look who's home," Troy said, sitting spread-legged on a kitchen chair with a beer in his hand.

"Where is she?"

"In bed, crying." Troy tipped back the beer. "You know the drill." He smiled, flexing his arms.

"Why, Troy?"

"Figure you owed me, brudda," he said, laughing. "How many beatings I took, defending your scrawny ass. For what? I didn't get nothing in the end. Your father Jewed me out my inheritance."

"I fought for you too," Bobby said. "I lost everything."

"Life's a bitch, ain't she? She's a real bitch in heat."

"So you fuck my wife? What kind of man are you?"

"You fucked my girl first, Bobby. Roxy told me all about you," Troy said. "You know what soldiers do to guys who mess with their girls while they're at war?" He picked a nail with the Randall knife.

"You didn't go to war, Troy."

"Hell I didn't," he said, "I shot enough Japs to fill a transistor radio factory."

"If you did all that from the brig in Pendleton, you're one hell of a shot."

Troy twisted his face into a sneer. "Big words from a pogue."

Karen lurked in the bedroom doorway, wearing a night shirt. Her hair lank, eyes red. "But he was shot by a sniper," she said. "He showed me the scars."

"Hush, Karen," Troy said. "Men are talking."

"Tell her, tough guy," Bobby said. "Show her the flip side to that Purple Heart. Let's see whose name is on it."

"Both of you go to hell," Troy said, sucking back the beer.

"You always took the easy way out," Bobby said. "Made me do your homework. So don't blame me 'cause you got booted out of school."

"Why? Because I wanted something I wasn't supposed to have?" Troy hollered, tossing the can in the corner. "Because I wasn't rich like you? I was trash from the other side of the tracks, and I'm supposed to be oh so grateful your old man took me in. You know what he did? He paid for my room and board with my inheritance, Bobby. Showed me the books. He even took fees for handling the money, like a damn leech. Left me with nothing. But you did my homework, huh? So what? There's nothing free in this world, and what you can't keep ain't yours—your old man taught me that."

Troy stood and stretched. "Like this dirty little girl of yours," he said, smiling. "She told me you found out, but she came crawling back this morning, Bobby. For what she needed. Hell, we did it again, right here, before you came home. All you gotta do is smack her around a little, and she warms right up."

Bobby leaped at him. Troy popped him in the chin, knocking his head back. He roared and bit Troy's forearm, throwing wild haymakers. Troy laughed and whipped a hook to Bobby's ear, sending him tumbling into the corner.

"Stop it!" Karen shouted.

"What? You love it. You told me yourself, you want a man who can defend what he's got."

Bobby stomped out the door.

"That's right, run you little coward," Troy called after him.

Bobby returned with the Luger and tugged the toggle joint to chamber a round. He raised the pistol as Troy hurled a chair at him, catching him in the face. The report rang in their ears, the gun smoke scent thick in the room. The round shattered a CorningWare dish on the stove.

Troy clamped his mitts on Bobby's hands, wrenching the pistol free. Karen hammered his back. "Stop hurting him!"

"Thanks, Bobby," he said, holding up the pistol. "This'll go good with the Iron Cross." He tucked it in the small of his back. "I'll be back tomorrow for your morning feeding, Karen."

Her lip trembled, and she kneaded the hem of her shirt, tugging it tight.

"You know, Karen. You are one red hot piece of tail. Look at her, Bobby. She needs it."

"What do you want?" Bobby moaned, clutching his wrist. "Just leave us alone."

Troy grinned, looking back and forth between them. "You gonna pay me to stop fucking your wife? That's rich," he said. "I like that. I dunno, Bobby. I like it. Not as much as she does, but I like it a lot."

Karen seethed, slumping against the wall in a pile.

"I'll take the Corvette," Troy said. "And you can keep the bike. The only thing she likes riding more than me." He grinned, flashing the chipped tooth. "We got a deal?"

Bobby slammed his elbow into the cabinets. "Take it, just go, and don't ever come back."

"See that, Red? You're not worth nothing, like you said. You're worth a brand new Corvette."

Troy strutted to the door.

"Wait," Karen husked through gritted teeth.

"One last time?" Troy kneaded his crotch. "The well is dry, honey."

"The race," she said, eyes rimmed red. "Bobby needs it for the race. You have to let us keep it until tomorrow."

"I don't gotta do nothing."

"Please, Troy."

He rubbed his stubbled chin. "You know what? I'm feeling generous. I'll meet you at the track. I'll even race for you. But gimme the keys. And the pink slip."

Bobby dug the keys from his pocket and threw them at Troy's jacket. "The pink's in the glove box."

"Now be nice, I'm doing you a favor."

"Thank you, Troy," Karen said.

"Anytime, Red. It was a blast." Troy laughed on his way out the door.

Bobby covered his face in his hands.

Karen crawled over to him and cradled his head to her chest as he shook. She led him to bed, untied his boots and tugged them off. She undressed him, tucked him in, and spooned behind, stroking his greasy black hair.

After he passed out, she tiptoed to the garage.

...

Bobby fired up the Corvette the next morning, his eyes dead. "She's running lean," he said.

"Let her be, baby." Karen rubbed the back of his neck. "She's not yours anymore."

Bobby looked down.

"I want to drive her one last time," Karen said.

She drove to the track like a grandfather heading to church. Her fingers stroking the sleek blue steering wheel, lingering on the chrome. She had her hair pony-tailed in a kerchief, big ruby-framed shades over her eyes.

"Let her loose," Bobby said.

She held a finger to his lips.

The track's black asphalt shimmered in the summer heat. Racers filled the lot, hoods down, shielding their secrets. Showroom queens, stripped roadsters, bulbous lead barges and sleek-finned sharks. Engines rumbled and the air tasted tangy with raw gas and burnt oil.

Bobby squeezed Karen's knee when he saw the Studebaker. The boys laughed and pointed.

"What, is the broad gonna drive?" Freckles said as they passed.

Troy waved from a spot in the grass. Karen downshifted and palmed the wheel, spinning the rear end out on the pavement in a perfect 180. Everyone stared, and Bobby patted her thigh. "Nice," he said.

Troy walked over. "Be easy with my wheels."

Karen killed the engine and tossed him the keys as she got out.

"She's yours, big boy. You drive her."

"We get three runs. If I'm rusty, you can drive." Troy grinned and climbed in the seat. "Best timeslip wins five hundred bucks. Maybe I'll split it."

Bobby held Karen's wrist. "I want to drive. It's my rep on the line."

"Let it go, baby," she whispered in his ear. "She's not yours anymore, but I am."

Bobby creased his brow, watching her. She folded her arms and stood high on wedge heels, collecting stares at his side.

A man with a clipboard walked down the line, approaching each driver. Bobby looked away when the man got to Troy to give him his number. Other racers came by to admire the silver blue rocket, whistling. Karen squeezed his hand.

Freckles and his pals strutted over, hollering from a distance. "You're up against me, little man. I'm gonna cream you."

Troy flicked a look, and they retreated, sending back sneers.

"Only thing that boy's gonna cream is his jeans," Karen said.

They watched cars pair up at the Christmas tree, the column of four lights that signaled the start. Blue, three sequential ambers, then green for go. The drivers smoked their tires to get them sticky, paired at the lines, and waited for the green. Squeals, then roars, faded into the distance as the cars vanished in the heat mirage down the quarter mile.

Bobby felt ripped from crotch to windpipe. "That orange T-bucket's gonna be the one to beat," he said to himself.

Troy smiled as the announcer called his number over the loudspeaker. "Gonna show 'em a real rod now, huh Bobby?" He climbed into the Corvette and fired up. The engine rumbled hard. Bobby felt the bass in his chest, dulling the ache.

Troy snapped his fingers. "Gimme a kiss, Karen. For luck."

Karen strolled over and planted one on his lips, eliciting whistles from the crowd. "Good luck, Daddy."

Troy smacked her on the behind and pulled away with a chirp of the tires. Karen returned to Bobby's side, draping her arm around his shoulders, giving him a squeeze. The Corvette rolled through the water box, and issued twin plumes of smoke as Troy lit up the tires. The Studebaker rolled next, fishtailing as the kid fed it too much pedal.

The light at the top of the tree glowed blue.

The engines spat and snarled.

Bobby hooked his arm around Karen's waist.

Amber one.

Two.

Three.

At the first glimmer of green, the engines howled, rising to a scream. They launched nose and nose, disappearing in a shriek of burning rubber. Bobby stood on tiptoe.

The Studebaker shot forward as they shifted into second.

Karen dug her nails into his shoulder.

The Corvette pulled away as they hit third, one length.

Bobby felt laughter rumbling out of his throat.

As they blasted into top gear, the Corvette rocketed away like a silver blue Sputnik, streaking past the finish. Bobby and Karen jumped and hugged, hooting with the crowd. Then the bottom fell out, as cheers turned to moans. Flames flickered bright in the Corvette's cockpit. The car swerved in front of the Stude, plowing into the safety wall. The kid driving the Studebaker panicked and cut hard, flipping end over end, spinning debris and driver into orbit.

The firemen scrambled to their truck and shooed the kids away. The Corvette burst in a silent fireball. A man of living flame tumbled out of the driver's seat, crawling from the wreckage. The crowd stared, hands saluting on their brows as they craned to see. Bobby dropped his arms to his sides, stumbling forward as the orange figure dragged itself across the asphalt and collapsed.

"You're not my Daddy no more," Karen whispered under her breath.

Bobby fell to his knees, tore up fistfuls of grass.

Karen threw a leg over the Indian and kicked it to life. She pulled up beside him and pushed her shoes into his hands.

"Hop on, baby," she said. "It's all over."

Bobby climbed on the back, clutching her waist.

"What happened?"

"We fixed him good."

Karen aimed the bike for the highway, and they took off down the long stretch of empty black road.

FORLORN HOPE
MATTHEW FUNK

Bayliss woke at 3am. Sharon slept, bare under his leather jacket like a tulip in a lake of oil. He left their Sandman Motel bed and went to the bathroom to give himself the look.

He could lose himself in the look. High, black slope of his duck-tail hair. Muttonchops trimmed with a straight razor. Shades' lens impenetrable as metal.

He looked at himself and saw wildness. Not haunted eyes. Not Corporal Don Bayliss, 8th Marines.

"I don't like it when people obsess over their appearance." Sharon stood behind him, slim as a scratch on a photograph and too serious for seventeen.

"I know."

He took her to bed.

...

"I especially don't like it when you do it."

He lit two Camel unfiltered from his USMC trench lighter. He passed one to her. Shot smoke from his nostrils. It billowed blue from Sharon, her pink lips garnished with tobacco flake.

"Why'd you wake?"

"Thinking," he said, because she was one of the two people he could admit that to.

"About what?"

"Killing your father."

...

Bayliss had stopped his Ford truck in Fond du Lac to steal a car.

He'd been riding from Albany to Detroit when he spotted a Cadillac with a bomber-wing design on its door. It made him pull over into an

Amoco and walk to the Elk Lodge where it was parked under a sycamore.

The Elk Lodge lot was vacant of people on Saturday mid-morning. He stood with hands in his skinny jeans, studying the lines of observation—lines of fire to Corporal Bayliss. He sneered at the design on the wide Cadillac side-panel.

The star was set in a circle of blue with white lashes: American Naval Air. For Bayliss, it was the eye of a God that laughed down at him.

He lifted the back of his jacket. Its custom design bunched—a flame of white around crimson letters, FORLORN HOPE. He drew out the slim jim from beside his switchblade.

Bayliss didn't steal for money. He stole for passion.

He'd taken a Yankees pennant off a house porch in Rochester. A pair of lucky dice from a drunken gambler in New Orleans. A radio from a general store in Denver.

The pennant, he'd floated on the Hudson River. The dice, down a rest stop toilet in Memphis. The radio, thrown off a mountain.

Bayliss slid the slim jim into the door panel.

He stole for the passion of the moment. That was the point. To take so that he could leave behind.

The Cadillac, he would steal for hate.

He hated its color, a celebration of sky blue. The skies had been blue above Saipan when the Jap mothers cut their children's bellies open and jumped off the cliffs by the dozens. He hated its chrome aerials and its winged fins. Wings had soared a world above him on Tinian, while below he ate smoke and tasted blood and starved. He hated its star and the smiling pin-up girl straddling it. The pin-up girls had smiled down over Tarawa for 76 unbroken hours of fear, explosions, and men screaming for mercy that never came and never would.

Bayliss yanked the slim too hard. It missed the lock and slipped free.

He aimed it again. The sound of boots on asphalt stopped him.

He turned to see a Sheriff approaching.

"Got business here, buddy?" The voice rid Bayliss of all his ready excuses. It sent him a decade back. Even under the hat brim, the Sheriff's squint was more familiar than the image Bayliss made in the mirror every morning.

"Maybe we'll just start with ID," the Sheriff said, seating hands on his gun belt. That belt was stretched around more gut than Bayliss remembered. But the haze gray hair that margined his square head was tight as ever. The same name, POTTER, was now stitched above a badge.

Bayliss kept silent in hope USMC Lieutenant Bob Potter wouldn't recognize him.

Potter hadn't missed a detail out of place for the three years Bayliss served in his command. He didn't now.

"Donnie?" Potter's squint narrowed. "That you under all that pomade?"

Potter smiled like he'd been waiting for twelve years to do it.

"Hey, Bob."

"Donnie Bayliss." The grin vanished, as if to help Bayliss recognize him better. The color kept glowing in his blockhouse cheekbones. "Son of a bitch. You've gone native."

"And you've held on to rank." This didn't surprise Bayliss. To Bob Potter, care and command were one in the same. Bayliss felt instinct straighten his spine as Potter inspected him.

"Shit, Donnie. Looks like you've seen too many Marlon Brando movies."

"And you've seen too much John Wayne."

Potter's nostrils flared. It was close as he ever got to a laugh. It made Bayliss smile despite himself.

"Looks must deceive me, though," Potter said. "I know you aren't messing with Big Russ' Caddy there."

Bayliss lost the smile. He used his lips to hold a cigarette instead.

Potter took Bayliss' pack and shook one out. Bayliss lit them both.

Potter exhaled with the sigh of a relapsed smoker.

"Jeanne still ride you about smoking around her furniture?" Bayliss spiked an eyebrow. Potter answered yes by saying nothing.

"You're in town to visit?" Potter said.

"Was planning on passing through."

Potter looked Bayliss over and nodded approval. But his mouth frowned all on its own and sped to say, "Why don't you stay for a bit?"

Bayliss' surprise showed less than Potter's.

"Catch up on old times," Potter said, rushing to rationalize while his features fell.

"Is that an order?"

"Yeah," Potter said, tossing the Camel on the ground and crushing it with his steel-toed boot. "Yeah, stay and we'll get a beer or two tomorrow."

"Yes," Bayliss said. He stopped himself from adding 'Sir' by dragging a hand over the greased plume of his hair instead.

The longer Potter stared, the more fright seeped into his bullet-point eyes. He turned, tugged his belt and ambled for the Elk Lodge.

"And stay away from the Caddy," Potter barked over his shoulder. "The big boy who owns it is one mean cuss. You should be less afraid of my jail and more afraid of him finding you."

Bayliss leaned on the Cadillac, jeans' seat over the girl's face, sneer releasing smoke. He'd given up fear ten years ago. He wasn't going back to it now.

...

Bayliss found his girl where he'd found himself—at the drive-in, among the youth.

Meeting Potter gave Bayliss an anxiety without an answer. It reminded him of the hunger he'd had as a child, bouncing with his father in a horse cart between garlic fields in California during the workless 30s. Weeks living on lard and flour created the kind of hunger that was even starved of healthy appetite.

He dropped a dime and a half on a hamburger and black coffee at Mae's Drive-In. It came with pickles, lettuce and tomato, and Bayliss realized he was still getting used to not having to pay extra for condiments.

He sat by the electric fan so that his pomade wouldn't sweat, and he watched the kids in the parking lot. They leaned or sprawled or bent on cars that were loud with color and engine. They shrugged in T-shirts and knee-skirts as if moving to a music all their own. Their cigarettes dangled at the corners of pouting mouths.

Bayliss paid more attention to them than to his burger. They were his people—his careless and rootless people. He had left the service, haunted at 18, and the speed of the youth had been his exorcism.

And though they were loud, their loudness was not the humbling volume of high-explosive hitting beach sand, or the snarl of diving planes, or the long screams of people burning to death.

Their sound burnt and boomed and lived. Their style celebrated itself.

He had adopted that style, that look, as his own.

The waitress frowned, false beauty mark sagging into her wrinkles, when he lit his fourth cigarette for his third cup of coffee.

"Going to have to pay more if you want more," she said as she poured. "Coffee's a nickel."

"You're paying for the table at this point."

Bayliss noticed no one else waiting for his space. He went to the jukebox to drown out the echo of the waitress.

Buried with Perry Como hits and Sinatra tunes were The Crew-Cuts. Bayliss selected "Sh-Boom." He cranked it.

He had only sat back down by the time the waitress stalked to the juke-box, turned it down and came to his table.

"I think you best leave."

"I'm a paying customer."

"You're a nuisance."

"I'll just wash up and be on my way, then."

He went to the bathroom with destruction on his mind: cracking their mirror, lodging towels in the toilet, pissing on the floor.

His nerves had been stitched with too many seconds spent unable to shoot back. He damn sure wasn't going to take fire without returning it. Not now. Not when he could put Fond du Lac, Bob Potter and that lard-and-flour feeling in his rearview mirror.

The girl almost collided with him coming out of the ladies' room.

"Pardon," she said, and the smile she put on was so practiced it could almost be mistaken as authentic.

Her makeup wasn't as good a mask. Bayliss spotted the purple corona of a bruise on her cheek under a bar of foundation. Lipstick couldn't hide the fresh split in her lip. The brittle edges of her eyes were evidence enough for Bayliss.

He'd seen the same in men, young and old, after their first day spent with Japanese metal slashing air, plants and people all around them.

He didn't move out of her way.

"Who did that to you?"

It took a while, the girl smiling and shaking her blond curls, before she copped to it.

"My old man."

"You going home to him now?"

"Not yet."

"That's what I would have told you."

She said her name was Sharon and he told her she could forget about home. That made her chin drop in a soft way that brought his hand to her elbow. He steered her to the truck, then steered the truck to a lakeshore where they could be alone.

Sharon didn't say much and neither did he. They listened to the radio and smoked cigarettes and nodded their heads together. Bayliss gave names to the birds on the lake and made up crazy stories about their love affairs to take her mind off the silence. When the bar of tension in her shoulders melted under his arm, he drew her to him.

She liked to stare, her face serious, more than she liked to kiss. She kissed with teeth.

He didn't hurry and she didn't say no.

That was enough for both of them to want to stay.

He left her outside her high school and took her phone number. She walked home and he drove to find a motel that charged by the week.

...

Potter picked Bayliss up at the Sandman Motel and seemed disappointed when Bayliss answered that he'd stayed out of trouble.

Potter told Bayliss about how the rest of F Company was living. Every story ended with a frown. He told Bayliss that he'd brought bologna sandwiches, but that they'd have to pick up their beers.

They wound up driving out of the dry county to get some whiskey. Potter's scowl only deepened as the night wore on, but he directed the whole thing. Bayliss only spoke up to agree with whatever Potter said. He just kept his hand out the window, skimming the wind, imagining it was a magic carpet Sharon and he could sail away on.

"Something wrong, Donnie?" Potter asked him after their second shot of whiskey. He said it with lips wrenched down, eyes like signal flares. Bayliss turned his attention from watching the highway by the campground they parked at.

"I could ask you the same, Potter."

"How about the whole damn world?" Potter didn't smile as he said it.

"Sounds about right to me."

"Nobody else gets that," Potter said, pouring another round of shots. His brow cinched like he was trying to squeeze something out of it. "Not even the guys at work. They watch people break the law every day, for no reason, but they don't really see people. Not like we've seen people."

Bayliss plucked his shot to wash away an image of a four-year-old Jap kid's face blistering as napalm bubbled through below. It worked. Just for an instant.

"They didn't serve like we did," Potter said. "Just a bunch of Army boys on ETO occupation duty or Signal Corps queers."

"No sense in trying to explain it, either," Bayliss said. It was why he didn't like talking to people; just talked at them. Potter nodded.

"A forlorn hope," he said, then swatted Bayliss' jacket. "Just like you got written right there. The suicide assault on the bunkers at Tarawa—the 'forlorn hope' mission. You can't forget that battle either, huh?"

"Can't forget any of them," Bayliss said, rolling his cigarette into the corner of his lips. "Can't do anything with it either."

Potter hung his head in thought. Bayliss listened to the highway, its sound like motion itself breathing. It blanketed the quiet between him and Potter, relaxing him.

"Maybe this is enough," Potter said, pulling from the whiskey and passing it to Bayliss. Their stares joined.

In that moment, and the hazy talk of fears and relief and sorrow that followed, Bayliss started to think Bob Potter might just be right.

This might be a place he could stay.

...

The Saturday matinee monster movie double feature was Bayliss' first real date with Sharon. She showed up ten minutes late without apology and he liked her more for it. They missed the newsreels and cartoons buying licorice and Cokes to go with the Old Crow in his hip flask.

They sat in the back row and watched Godzilla destroy Tokyo through blue tides of cigarette smoke. His hand was restless in the valley of her knee-length skirt. She traced the words FORLORN HOPE on his jacket, spilled her fingers over the atomic-white flames as if trying to hold onto them.

Bayliss liked Godzilla. The big lizard had the right attitude. War had revived him and he wrecked the tidy department-store-box cities in reply. All the shrieking Japanese people made him nervous, though.

He admitted that to Sharon when she noticed his Camel shaking between his fingers. "Guess I just don't like seeing people afraid."

Something in her features softened. She lost the smile but the look she got was prettier without it. She kissed his knuckles, his ember by her cheek, until they calmed.

His pinky finger traced her jaw.

"No new bruises," he said.

"Not yet," she said, and her look didn't change. It stayed, soft and patient and open to him.

"Maybe I should straighten your old man out."

"They don't come straighter than him."

He didn't push it. Something would have to be done about her old man, if he was going to stay. But for now, just staying was enough.

Under the sun and marquee of theater, the world around seemed washed out, vanished into spotlights focused on them. Here, he had the scent of licorice and lipstick on his hand; he had her eyes giving themselves to his; he felt born into this moment, peace without prologue.

Here, he wanted to stay.

It scared him. Bayliss turned and kicked an empty popcorn box. Better to bring it all down and be on his way, before it brought him down like Godzilla.

He looked back to Sharon, already thinking of what he'd say when he left her.

She had walked a few steps away and was staring at a car parked on the curb.

The Cadillac spread in front of the theater, gleam like a weapon under the sun.

"Let's go inside," Sharon said and did.

Bayliss didn't watch the next film, *Them!*, much. He watched Sharon. He studied the blond of her hair and wondered if Big Russ was blond too.

She just stared at the screen.

When a little girl, catatonic with shock, was interrogated by Army men onscreen, Sharon leaned forward in her seat. Her hands were fists that hid in her lap.

The little girl onscreen began to shriek.

Sharon got up and walked for the door.

Bayliss found her in the parking lot, vomiting by the dumpsters.

Hearing his engineer boots clicking behind her, she righted herself. Arranged her curls into a bounce. Fixed her lipstick. Put on her look.

Her smile was full when she finally turned to him. Her eyes were hollow.

"I need to go soon," she said.

He felt the fist he'd kept in his chest 10 years open and reach out.

He knew then that he would stay. He knew this was love.

•••

Sunday was dinner at Potter's.

Bayliss had accepted the invitation drunk. He had every intention of treating it like most of his drunken promises, blowing it off without a second thought.

Instead, he pulled up to Bob Potter's manicured lawn with an appetite. The scent of what he'd done with Sharon after the movie perfumed his truck cab. It gave him a hunger he could trust—for food, for people, for a place.

Potter had made quite the place for himself: Plastic daisy pinwheels raised from buzz-cut grass, real flowers dozing in bloom in front of a white-washed porch, American flag asleep in the evening heat.

The ingrained urge to steal something slept too, beneath a lifting feeling—a possibility that maybe one day he could have this. He and Sharon could.

He could be a foreman for a field crew, managing men like his father as they picked pumpkins or corn or succotash for him. He could work cars. He could build something.

He could build them something.

He took in the sight of the house and the smell of trimmed plants a moment too long. He noticed the Cadillac parked a few houses down in a driveway across the street.

The house was as blue as the Caddy. Bayliss wondered which window was Sharon's. He thought of her looking out it at the street, doing her hair as she dreamed of the roads that street could lead to.

"Donnie," Potter called, stepping from the opening door onto the porch. He had a high-ball glass in hand, waved Bayliss to him with the other. "Come on in. It's even nicer inside."

It was.

Potter had the whole place shining, had roast-beef aroma in the air, had silver on the table and gilding the ashtrays and gleaming from picture frames on the wall. He had Jeanne laying food on the table, and she wiped her hands on a spotless apron before coming over to grab Bayliss' shoulders.

She looked him over, doe-eyed above a tense smile.

"Donnie Bayliss," she said, then squeezed his arms. "I always thought you'd be shorter."

"I was."

Potter laughed as if he'd won the lottery, big and booming.

"What's with all this, though?" Jeanne said, reaching up to scrub his hair. Bayliss pulled back in time to save its high crest.

"He just hasn't been in town long enough to get a haircut," Potter said, steering them both for the table. "He's been busy settling in."

Bayliss realized Potter was right. Settling in had been accidental, but that was Bayliss' way—careening around the past 10 years, life had just been one hit-and-run after the next. Now he had reason to park.

Potter gave Bayliss a firm look that told them both he knew he was right. It reassured Bayliss. Potter had been right about a lot during the war. Between life and death, he'd chosen right for Bayliss the whole way through.

Bayliss shrugged into the seat he was assigned—across from the head of the table—and figured he would let Potter be right about this, too.

"Get you a drink?"

"Sure. What're you having?"

"Iced tea."

"I'll have one of those."

Bayliss shelled a pistachio from the bowl on the table. He ate it while Jeanne stared. He stared back, a feeling of comfort only growing. She felt familiar to him. It was as if the letters Potter had carried, creased and swept clean of island dirt, were gathering to form her features.

"Bob says you like roast beef."

"My old man used to call it the dinner of kings. Said Henry VIII had it with every meal."

"That's what Bob said."

Her smile came easier this time. Bayliss returned it.

He was still smiling as Potter pivoted him around by his shoulder.

"Let me introduce my princess," Potter said, waving a hand toward the girl who stood rigid in a knee-skirt and blond curls beside his bulk.

It took all Bayliss had not to let his smile fracture.

"This is Sharon."

...

Bayliss' plan was simple:

Wednesday, he'd meet Sharon at Walgreens. They'd shop separately.

Potter had always told him, whether it was a ten-meter-high heap of dirt or an entire airfield they had to seize: Keep It Simple, Stupid. The KISS Principle.

Sharon would buy some food with her own money. Bayliss would cover the toiletries, clothes and road atlases.

Bayliss had been an enlisted man—a sniper—not an officer. His job was to hit and move, hit and move before detection. Keeping it simple suited him fine.

"He'll kill you if he finds out," Sharon had whispered to Bayliss, picking up dessert plates, during the one time they'd been left alone on Sunday dinner.

"He won't find us."

"He doesn't mess around," she'd said, voice scurrying. "Him and that Russ buddy of his—the things they've done to troublemakers, the things they laugh about at their poker games as I listen in bed—they don't mess around."

"He can't find what he can't catch."

She'd given him her eyes then, and though they were afraid, they weren't fleeing Bayliss. They were reaching out.

"I run better than anybody alive," he told her.

So the plan was to meet at the Walgreens. Then get in his truck and get her lost, somewhere between when she was at flute lessons and when she was supposed to be at Mae's Drive-In. They would go to the Sandman Motel, until Potter got off his night shift, and then they would go to the highway.

Bayliss couldn't sleep Wednesday night. He tried to exhaust himself in Sharon's body. It only left him more anxious.

After she caught him readying his look in the mirror, she'd fallen back to sleep while trying to soothe him with caresses. He laid his leather jacket over her. She curled her arm from across his chest, bunching the jacket close about her, its FORLORN HOPE lettering a yoke around her neck.

He stared at the window until he saw light hatch from under the curtain.

Then he went to pack the truck.

He had just finished stowing the picnic basket under the passenger seat when a baton crashed across his skull.

Bayliss went blind. He knew he was on the ground because he could hear boots on the concrete around his ears. He tried to remember the last time he'd been knocked out, sought some context, thought it was probably Saipan, but this didn't smell like Saipan. Saipan smelled like flowers and high-octane-fuel burn.

Here smelled like Burma-Shave and boot leather.

The thought of Sharon brought his blood rushing enough to clear his vision.

Bob Potter stood aside his head. On the other side was a stocky man with sandy hair and granite hands. The hands rubbed, restless like the circling wolves Bayliss would watch nights up in Napa while his father slept in a shack with no door.

"Get this straight, Donnie," Potter said. He put a boot sole on Bayliss' mouth, barricaded it, ground grit into gums and lips. "You're going to wake up tonight. But only because I owe you just that. You get to live, because you made sure I did."

Potter straightened. The boot sank. Gums split.

"You're going to wake up and you're going to run along and keep running," Potter said.

He was hardly done talking when Big Russ began jumping on Bayliss' ribs.

...

Bayliss spent 9 days and 34 nickels reaching Sharon. He leaned against the Appleton payphone by the record store and waited for a boy in the Mae's Drive-In parking lot to get her on the line. Her voice came through hard like a scab.

It was a lot of "fine" and "nothing wrong" from her. That lasted three minutes until she began to cry.

For Bayliss, things had not been fine. Every other thought since he dragged his bruises into the truck cab and drove north had been of her preciousness: the contours of her neck, the lilt she got when talking about rock bands or movie stars or seeing the ocean, the tension in her hands, the way her eyes were either frozen or restless—never in between, the "hello" she had that made everything that came before seem a lifetime away.

Bayliss didn't know how he could live without that "hello" starting things over right for him.

His other thoughts were of Potter.

"How bad did he get?" Bayliss asked her, pressing his brow to the payphone's cover until it made an angry red line.

Sharon just cried.

"How bad?"

He thought on Potter beating her, belting her, locking her in the closet—all the things she'd told him about that night at the Sandman.

"I'll get you out of there, Sharon."

"There is no out," she said. "He's told me he'll never let me leave. Not until I'm old enough. Not until I've met a man to marry. Which means, not ever."

"You met me and that's enough."

Sharon laughed the very same way Bayliss had heard dying men laugh.

"You're not enough." She'd stopped crying. She was cold and numb and rigid, and Bayliss remembered that happening to many he loved too.

"You never were. There's nothing you can do."

He hung up on her. He walked Appleton. He walked just to keep moving.

He passed soda fountain counters and department stores and drive-ins—Appleton was a small town like all the other small towns that Bayliss ran from and to in endless succession.

It reminded him that there was one thing he could not run from.

He sold his jacket to a pawn shop. He didn't even trace the letters, FORLORN HOPE, a final time—just handed it over while making sure his shades covered his black eyes.

He spent the money on the only solution he knew.

...

Bayliss tracked the movements of the men coming in and out of the Fond du Lac Elk Lodge. They passed beneath streamers hung on the awning and milled by a cooler of Kool-Aid set on a picnic table out front. From the ridge 500 meters distant, he couldn't hear them laugh, just see their plump bodies shake and their lips pull wide.

He resented these men.

They grew fat hurrying in the same circles, job to house to lodge to house to job. They held onto their little world so hard that they broke it. They felt entitled to the damage they did.

Some kids were there, but Bayliss paid them no notice. Some things had to be blocked out. He looked down the .30-06 Springfield's scope for Bob Potter alone.

Waiting brought the heat, wet as a dog's mouth. His hair swamped his head. Flies crawled in the sunburn blooming on his unjacketed back.

He blocked these out too. He blocked it all out: The laughter, the kids, the heat, the music, the look, the war.

All those things would and could pass. Even the life as Sharon's lover could and had been taken from him.

Bob Potter stepped from the Elk Lodge and screened his narrow eyes from the sun.

Bayliss let him live two seconds longer. Enough to draw a bead on his head.

He made that head vanish with a squeeze of the trigger.

Potter dropped to his knees and pitched back. And the people around him scattered like sheep, just like they always had when Bayliss took one of their number, even though it wouldn't save them for long. It was nothing new to Bayliss.

Only one person rushed to Potter.

Sharon threw herself to her father's side.

She grabbed his shirt and tried to lift him. She turned her face away from the absence of Potter's. Between a ring of tears, her mouth wrenched wide at the sky.

Bayliss knew the look well. She was begging for something that was already gone.

He left the ridge at a walk. There was no sense in running. Time and towns and things he took would all pass by.

The one thing that could not be taken from him was that he was a killer.

He wept for Sharon but had no hope left in him to pray for her.

ONLY THE VULTURES WILL SEE ME HANG
NIK KORPON

The last thing Charlie says before Butch takes the door is, "You fuck this one up, I'll shoot you myself."

Butch nods. "Mom always said you were the practical one." Then he pulls the red bandana over his mouth and shoulders the door open.

The clerk behind the counter doesn't move, just keeps his eyes on the sports section of the *Kansas City Star*, rereading the account of Don Larsen's gem in the Series. Not that it matters too much which team wins the crown; if it's not his Athletics, he doesn't rightly care. Still, a perfect game in the World Series is a thing to behold. He's turning to page four when the column bulges. Folding down the edge shows him nothing but the barrel of a gun.

Butch motions to the cash register with his Mauser and drops a canvas bag on the counter. "I think you understand how this goes."

Charlie keeps watch at the door, black bandana covering his mouth and a finger wrapped around the trigger. He hates wearing these bandanas because he can smell his own breath in them, but it's better than offering up his portrait to a nimble-minded clerk who has a way with pencil and paper. Hell, it's not really that bad. Definitely not like some of the huts he'd cleared before razing during his tour over in the islands. Shit, piss, blood, vomit. A pile of human decay beside a bassinet. How those animals could live like that isn't something he's sure he ever wants to understand, but the bomb fixed a lot of their problems. Fixed them up in a flash.

Problems, though, that's what the clerk is having with his register. He told his old man that the drawer kept sticking but his old man wasn't willing to put out the money to get a new one. Put some elbow grease in it, he'd said. That was the problem with kids today, he'd said. The clerk's shaking hands don't help in working the busted machine open either. He's heard stories about men like these two before, but they were usually from his old man and the story ended with the robber swallowing Dad's Remington 31. That's all they'd been, though—stories. Now, with this bandana-man tracing his outline with a pistol and his hands shaking like after he saw Miss Monroe in that scene in *The Seven Year Itch*, he wished his old man would stop telling the story. And the whole time, the man with the red bandana keeps pointing his gun and going on in that dirty Okie drawl about how Brooklyn definitely can't win the Series now. Damn vagrants, the clerk thinks as the register finally dings open.

"I'll take a cup of joe when you're done," Butch says, pointing at the coffee pot. "I'd pour it myself but I don't want to take away your livelihood."

Charlie coughs into his hand, stares at Butch like he's saying, What'd I tell you outside?

"Make it sweet and blonde, the way I like my trim."

The clerk can't see him smiling behind that bandana, but he can sure hear it. He scoops money from the till and dumps it in their bag. The canvas is the color of a bruised olive, the stains ranging from deep red to black. As he's giving away the money they needed to pay the bank this month, the man with the black bandana strides across the room. The clerk can't hear what they're saying, but it doesn't sound pleasant.

"I've got this under control," Butch says.

"Like hell." Charlie tries to scratch his cheek but the damn bandana is in his way like always. "In and out. That's our way. What'd I tell you outside?"

Butch cocks his gun and points it at his own face. "Go 'head, if you're needing to. But I need some coffee before we set out again. Didn't get good sleep last night."

"Then stop dreaming." Charlie places a palm on Butch's gun, lowers it, then turns and points his M1911 at the clerk. "We'll be leaving now."

The clerk nods, his lips quivering and making his words shake. "Do you still want coffee?"

"No."

"Yes."

Charlie turns to face Butch the way a shadow chases a sundial. "We'll be going now."

"I told you I'm tired. I need some coffee before we ride, unless you want me to crash my bike."

Butch leans back against the wooden service counter, which is fortunate for him because Charlie rotates through the punch the way his CO taught him back in Luzon—some spittoon of an island in the Philippines he couldn't find unless he had a compass pointed at Hell—and knocks Butch clear off his feet, the counter being the only thing holding him up. Charlie grabs him under the armpits to hoist him to standing, whispers, "No details and no wasted time means no jail time," then pushes him toward the front door, grabbing the canvas bag on the way.

Standing before the clerk, Charlie extends his hand, lets the metal barrel rest on the end of the kid's nose. "What's your name, son?"

"Tim."

"You think about calling for help, Tim, I'll know."

Tim shakes his head.

"You do, I'll string you up by your ankles and bleed you out from the throat."

He pushes the door open and steps right into Butch's back, and before he can open his mouth, he hears a slurred voice yelling to put their hands up. Charlie steps once around Butch, takes a knee and puts three bullets in the deputy's car. Shattered glass falls to the ground, a small dust-storm from the rushing hole in the front left tire. The deputy shouts but his voice is muffled, ducked into the front seat like he is.

Charlie pushes Butch towards their bikes. He slips his arms through the bag's straps and throws a leg over his Indian then looks over at Butch. "This is why we don't stay for coffee."

Butch rubs his jaw beneath the bandana. "See you there."

The bikes' tires throw rocks behind them, and leave a cloud of dust to drift over the dirt parking lot.

...

Charlie doesn't believe that Korea was actually a war and so he feels he has no point of comparison with Butch. Butch says that The War to End All Wars was spread over two continents, and though his older brother's men did their country a great service, they weren't surrounded by water on three sides. All that death was distilled into one small country full of farmers and villages and peasants riding animals. It's not the amount of blood spilled, Butch thinks, it's the thickness of that blood, how hard it is to wash from your face. Charlie can't tell him that he understands being trapped by water. Those long months in the Philippines, watching the kamikazes fall like damned stars, smelling the burning gas and flesh, picking up a tree branch to clear away some jungle and not realizing it's a charred arm until the wedding band flashes in the sunlight, they come to him in quiet moments, in loud moments, in dark and light and no matter if his eyes are open or shut, they come to him. So no, Charlie can't tell his younger brother he understands being trapped by water because he can't tell him anything about that island at all.

But both of them can agree they've slept beneath too many open moons and won't spend a night without a roof over their head and a mattress beneath their bodies.

They arrive at the motel separately, Charlie at dusk and his brother a good forty minutes after the sun disappeared. Butch veered east once they got out of Bonner Springs, in the off-chance the deputy had a buddy within radio-distance. Before every job, they decide which direction they're heading. Once that's settled, the rest is easy: third town on the highway, third motel in the town. When they started robbing, Charlie'd wanted to go further away. That was easy when they were working back east, but out here, the fifth town might not be until the next state, and who knows if that one will even have six motels. West has seemed the best direction and they plan to go that way until they reach Arizona, then tack back across the country before touching the coast. They've spent too much time near the water and want to keep their feet dry.

Butch walks into the motel room and finds Charlie stubbing out a cigarette then lighting another. There have to be a dozen butts in the blue glass ashtray.

"That was foolish, back there." Charlie doesn't look up when he speaks.

"Everything was fine." Butch shrugs off his leather jacket. "Didn't even fall asleep on the road."

"Little things like that are going to get us a reservation in the gas chamber."

Butch plops down on the bed. The springs squeak. He pulls off his boots, places the Mauser inside the right one. "No one's catching me, brother. Only the vultures will see me hang."

A cloud of smoke leaks from Charlie's lips. He rubs his brow then rises with a deep sigh, walking across the worn carpet to the map splayed out on the desk. "A couple more jobs and we'll be in the desert. Might get your wish if you keep that up."

"I worked my way through more firefights over there than any of these hillbillies can manage. You just worry about yourself."

Charlie looks up from the map. "I am."

He goes back to his bed but doesn't lie down. Can't really lie down anyway. His body is screaming for some rest but his brain can't see fit to cooperate.

Butch, though, his eyelids are already twitching. Didn't even take his shirt off before giving up. It's a skill learned in the Army, coveted in the Army, and possibly the reason he adjusted to civilian life as well as he has, being able to sleep. Rather, as well as he ever has. Besides being well-insulated from snipers, driving a Sherman through the hills had its advantages in that during the downtime, he already had a place to sleep.

Pacing the edge of the room, Charlie puts one foot in front of the other. Heel, toe. Heel, toe. For a throbbing second, he's back on night watch, letting the men of his platoon catch a few. Letting his ears relax to the rhythm of the jungle, determining the difference between a bird landing on a branch and a child's foot landing on a twig. He was never sure if the night watch was punishment or a blessing, allowing his mind to focus on jungle sounds instead of flashburn images.

The platoon had been clearing a village, making sure there were no civilians before they brought out the gasoline and cigarettes. Charlie held watch with his Grease Gun, scouring the tree line for any incomings while the other men went from hut to hut. He'd heard a woman screaming, and as he spun saw his CO backpedal out of a hut, a Filipino woman banging her fists on his chest. Charlie'd called out for her to lower her arms, to step away calmly, indicating with his gun where to move. She continued, and as Charlie took sight to fire a warning shot, he saw a thin ghostly girl step out of the doorway, a stuffed rabbit clutched in her stained hand. Seeing a white girl was odd, but Christian missionaries had been in the islands for years. The part that froze Charlie was the girl's eyes, something he could describe only as shocking blue, the same color as his daughter's. Like she'd stolen his daughter's soul and brought it to this hellish place just to remind him of what he was missing at home.

It wasn't until he began to lower his gun that he realized the zipping sound he heard wasn't his life being sucked out through his feet, but two grenades flying past him. They bounced once then all he saw was white.

When his eyes cleared, he couldn't tell which limbs belonged to which man. A leg lay beside him, ribbons of flesh draped across the jungle floor. He set the blade of his field knife between his teeth, bit down and dislodged the chunk of wood sticking out of his leg. He tore off a length of the pants to wrap around his own calf and staunch the bleeding. Later in the hospital tent, he remembered thinking it looked like the grip of a baseball bat when a pitcher cuffs a batter and the bat shatters. Holding the wood in his hand, he leaned back to take a long breath and saw the girl with the rabbit slinking along the tree line, his daughter's eyes six thousand miles from home, staring at him as they receded into the dark of the jungle. He grabbed the M1911 lying on the ground, peeled back the fingers of his CO and dropped the dead man's severed hand, then started searching for his daughter's soul.

When he got home, his wife never could get used to Charlie pacing, trying to stamp out the aura of that girl. She'd hear the clicking all night long, like some grandfather clock carved just to drive her mad. It could've been one of the clocks he'd sold at the Carver's Furniture in town before the war, the ones she'd sold when he was touring the Pacific, the ones she continued selling after he got back because her math was better and her personality both relaxed women and attracted men. Losing the job only pushed him further away from her, pushed him closer to his bottles, pushed his arm back farther when it swung at her. It happened only once, but as she spun around, her mouth kissing the edge of the kitchen table, he heard a muted shriek and turned to see his daughter standing in the doorway, her stuffed Velveteen Rabbit clutched in her hand, her shocking blue eyes staring at her mother's mouth, now dripping red. Charlie removed himself from the house the next day.

Butch's voice startles him. He turns and sees Butch sitting up in bed, smoking a cigarette.

"Try to close your eyes for ten minutes." He points at the window, sunlight streaming around the edges of the wool curtains. "We've got to work today."

...

Deputy Lindsey Ryan stretches out his back and crooked leg when he steps from the car into the gravel parking lot of Levins' Diner. Ten hours of driving in a Buick will wreak havoc on a man's back. He'd've rather had his patrol car, but Tim's old man isn't the world's most acute businessman and didn't have neither a spare tire nor a patch kit in the garage. Ryan had to call his wife at home and get her to bring their car to the gas station, baby and all, then take her home before setting out to track down those two motorbiking sons of bitches. Figures now's a good time to get some eggs and coffee, refuel his tank before setting out again.

He tips his hat to his uncle sitting at the counter, then waves to the waitress and shuffles over to a booth, loping his bent leg onto the bench. He sets his wide-brim on the table by his hands as she comes over.

"Two eggs, over easy, two sausages and some toast, if you don't mind. I like my coffee hot and full, darling." He nods. "Obliged."

The woman dings the bell behind the wooden counter. A little head peeks eyes over the booth's edge, stares at Ryan. They remind him of pictures he saw in *Life Magazine* after the war, of the brilliant blue water around the islands where men fought. He twists his lips up and she giggles. Her mother tells her not to bother the nice man and her face disappears.

...

"I hope I don't need to say it," Charlie says. "That we've reached an understanding."

"Let's just get this done, okay? I'm hungry." Butch pulls the red bandana over his mouth, cocks his Mauser.

Only three of the eight booths inside are full. One man sits at the counter shoveling oatmeal in his mouth. When the woman leaning into the kitchen turns around, her trembling lips shatter the welcoming smile.

"Hello, darling," Butch says. "Let keep this friendly, okay?"

Charlie sweeps the room with his pistol, watching for anyone who's feeling brave. The man in the back booth watches them with a dumbfounded intensity. Charlie cocks the pistol, lets the click of metal on metal ring out.

The canvas bag lands with a thud on the counter. Butch nods at the bag then sidles up to the oatmeal man, asks how the food is here. The man grunts, though whether he doesn't want to insult the cook or he's trying to avoid contact with an armed man, Butch can't tell.

He points at the purple scar that runs from the man's temple down under his jawline, lets out a little laugh. "You tell her the pot roast was dry or she catch you with the neighbor woman?"

The man clears his throat, grumbles, "Kaiser's bayonet. Didn't see him coming."

Charlie calls out, "An understanding, right?"

Butch extends his arm and shakes hands with the scarred man. "You're a good man. Thank you."

He turns to check on the woman's progress when Charlie yells, "Keep your ass planted unless you want to be breathing through your neck."

Butch spins around with his gun extended, clocks the man in the back standing up and raising his hands. Charlie yells to sit down again, and Butch feels a hot flash spread through his torso. He wobbles on his feet, catches a glimpse of the scarred vet rearing back for another kidney punch and squeezes his eyelids like fists.

A bang, his ears ringing.

He opens his eyes and sees a squirt of blood coming from the vet's shoulder, turns and sees Charlie pointing his pistol in their direction, turns and sees the man in the back booth raise a gun at Charlie. Butch pulls his trigger four times and the man splashes blood over the vinyl booth.

There's a thin shriek, a whimper, a death-stare from Charlie to Butch, Charlie shaking his head and sighing then popping two shots, taking three steps, popping another two shots. The waitress who greeted them collapses into a pile at Butch's feet, the cook slumps over the divide between kitchen and dining room. Blood and flesh sizzle on the grill, and the smell fills the air. Neither Charlie nor Butch notice.

Butch works himself to standing, rubbing blood back through his torso.

"No witnesses," Charlie says to him. "So no chamber."

Butch nods, hobbling over to the counter to grab the canvas bag. He wants to say it was an extreme reaction, to say that maybe the other patrons didn't strike him as heroes and they didn't need to die. But breathing is painful and his ribs are throbbing and he's just tired, so instead he slings the bag over his shoulder and makes his way toward the door.

He looks to Charlie and says, "That was a kind woman you just shot."

And over his brother's shoulder, Butch catches a glimpse of a stuffed rabbit hanging from the vinyl seat of a booth, its arms waving like it's trying not to plummet to its death on the ceramic tile below.

"Dear God." Butch drops the bag and hurries to the booth, pushing Charlie aside. "You cold-hearted son of a bitch."

Charlie barely looks up, just thumbs more bullets into the mag.

Using the seat back to lower himself, Butch kneels down.

There's a quick gasp, a slight whimper snuffed. There's blood dripping from the tabletop above, landing in a baseball-sized puddle. There's a young girl burying her head between her knees, rocking back and forth. Her feet sit but two inches from the dark red circle.

"Come here, sweetheart." Butch holds out his hand. He can practically hear her shaking. "Come on, let's get you out of here." He reaches out to touch her, and she yelps. "Just hold my hand and keep your eyes closed. I'll get your bunny for you."

His pulse throbs against his temples, against his ribs. His veins feel ready to tear themselves to shreds. His fingers tremble until he's sure they'll shake loose, but his body stills when she wraps her right hand around his. She leans forward, feeling with her left hand. Butch grabs that one too, about three chin hairs from her plopping it in her mother's blood.

A faint vibration comes from her mouth, an attempt at words or sobs.

"It's going to be okay, sweetheart. Let's go find you some ice cream."

A click behind him. He doesn't turn, just says, "Put that down, brother."

"No witnesses," Charlie says. "No chamber."

"She's a damn kid." Butch pulls her from underneath the table and sets her on his knee. He looks up and can't quite comprehend the look on his brother's face—shock, revulsion, terror, love—but he understands the source. Butch and Charlie didn't exchange many of their jungle stories, but after a job in Louisville took a particularly nasty turn, they drowned it out with two bottles of Kentucky moonshine. The story of the soul-stealing girl and her explosive tendencies came spilling out in something Butch thought to be alcohol-induced exorcism. Seeing this girl now, it's like coming home from a tour and catching first glimpse of your family on the porch, only to register that the buzzing in your ears isn't residue from the war but a plane diving right into your yard.

"No witnesses," Charlie repeats. He motions with the barrel.

"It ain't her," Butch says. "Go on out to the bikes. I'll take care of this."

The gun stays trained on the little girl's forehead. The girl trembles so hard it make Butch's leg wobble. Butch extends a hand, slowly as he would to a poised snake, and nudges Charlie's hand away.

Charlie pulls the trigger three times. Plumes of vinyl and stuffing and grey fur fill the air. The rabbit's ruined carcass falls to the floor. Charlie spins on his heels and heads to the front, stopping to grab the bag, then slams the door.

Butch stands and adjusts the girl in his arms. "What's your name, sweetheart?"

Her voice is muffled by Butch's shoulder, but it sounds like Sadie.

"Sadie, I'm Maynard, but my friends call me Butch. That there was my brother, Charlie."

She pulls her face back, and he can get a look at her features. A tow-headed waif of a girl, not more than five or six. Faint copper freckles that seem borrowed from one of her friends, and eyes a color that he'd only seen on Charlie's daughter, Dell. He tucks her hair behind her ear and says they should get going.

When they step outside Levins' Diner, he plops her on his Harley and saddles up behind her, then takes off his jacket and ties the arms around the both of them.

"Just hold on tight," he tells her.

"Why are you on motorbikes?"

"You ever tried to hide a Buick with a couple tree branches?" He kick-starts the engine, opens the throttle a bit.

"We don't have a car."

Butch nods. "Exactly."

...

Something about that smell throws Edgar back a few years. He can hear the frantic screech of foreign birds, of voices screaming in guttural tongues. He remembers learning to tell the difference between a hops field and a wheat field when it's burning, you have to breathe deep and watch the smoke. He remembers one of the other infantry saying it was hard to tell because sometimes the farmers trapped in the field put out their own smell while on fire. In his mind, they knew what was coming and should've moved faster and, if they didn't, well, there's one for Darwinism.

Edgar pulls himself up using one of the counter stools. The burn spreads through his shoulder, causing his fingers to loosen and slip from the stool's back. He catches himself before falling back to the floor, pulls through the pain until he finds his feet. Applying a little pressure around the wound tells him it's an in-and-out and blood loss is the only real thing to worry about.

The restaurant is not a world for the living. Poor Irma's piled not three feet from him, blood radiating from her like a gruesome sunset. He shoulders open the door to the kitchen, finds Big Al slumped across the griddle. Wrapping his good arm around the big man's waist, he heaves him back, off the steaming griddle. Blood burnt black, pocked with bubbles. The front of Al's torso looks like the remains of a campfire the morning after a rain. Edgar grabs a spatula meant for flipping burgers and sets it on the steel, then searches through the kitchen for a towel or rag. Only ones he sees are hanging from the edge of the sink, soaked with grease water, so he pulls off Al's hat and rolls it into a cylinder. He takes a deep breath then sets it between his teeth and picks up the spatula.

It's been a long time since he's heard that sizzle. At least he doesn't have to worry about getting Kraut disease in it this time.

When his shoulder is cauterized, he makes his way back through the dining room over to the back booth. His nephew lies face down on the table, a corona of blood ebbing toward the edge.

Damn shame, that kid. Bad enough his momma named him Lindsey and gave him clubbed feet. And now, shot down like a stray dog.

Edgar'd tried to do right by his sister's boy. He wanted to follow in his uncle's footsteps and fight the good fight, but he was kept out of the service on account of his palsy. Edgar had a few friends round town and did some favors to get the boy a badge and a gun, give him something to inspire a bit of respect.

He kneels down and closes the boy's eyelids, then takes the car keys from his pocket and walks outside.

...

Butch pulls the blanket up to Sadie's chin and secures it beneath her shoulders. She doesn't look terribly comfortable, but it's the same way he's seen mothers tuck in daughters in the pictures. Though he always wanted kids that he could play baseball and wrestle with, his old lady was more concerned about her ladies' club and themed dinners than procreating. When he got back from Korea and found her closet empty, he'd have to think of the bodies of infantry he left behind to bring about the necessary response when asked how he was doing. Taking up the road with Charlie was as simple as leaving his front door open. He cinches the wool blanket tighter around his own shoulders, the chill of riding without a jacket in damp air still lodged inside him.

Butch and Sadie passed the limits of the second town an hour after leaving the diner, and the third town shimmered like a mirage on the flat horizon of the plains. It perpetually grew on the straightaways, while at the same time receding into the distance when the road curved. The rain began twenty miles out. At first it only spat down on them and they could manage, but fell harder each time their wheels turned and Butch had to pull off into a copse of trees to keep her from the weather. By the time they finally parked around the corner from the Shangri-La Motel half a day later, Charlie had filled the room with thick cigarette smoke.

"I can't sleep without Gabby," Sadie says. Her eyes are dry but continually dart around the room, following Charlie's circuit.

"You shouldn't call your momma by her first name, darling."

"Gabby's my rabbit."

Butch nods. He looks around, scanning the room for anything to take Gabby's place. Pulling the pillowcase off the extra pillow, he folds it twice then ties a knot, emulating a vague head and flowing body, then hands it to her.

"That's not Gabby."

"It's either that or my socks." He pats her cheek and says to sleep. She closes her eyes but Butch can see the twitch beneath her eyelids, still tracing Charlie's movement.

Charlie grabs Butch's arm, yanks him up and pushes him out the door to the carport.

"Two guns, two bikes, two beds." The cherry of Charlie's cigarette flickers bright red, the same color of his cheeks as he sucks in hard.

"You don't sleep anymore, so it's not really an issue."

"When did you become the keeper of the poor?"

"Her daddy died over in Korea, and you took off her mom's face on a humbug. What else should I do?"

Charlie scoffs. "How do you know anything about her daddy?"

"I asked her."

He just shakes his head, mutters something about gallows. "I think it'd be wise to lay low for a few days and let the dust cover our tracks. Figure out how to get rid of that kid."

Butch takes the cigarette from Charlie's mouth and throws it on the ground, crushes it with the toe of his boot. "You can bunk up with me if your legs get tired, but keep quiet. Girl needs her sleep."

He opens the door and motions for Charlie to go in first, holds a finger to his lips that Charlie ignores. Butch lets the door whisper closed then crosses the room and sinks into the empty bed with a long sigh. He can hear Sadie's breath ebb and flow. When he tried to take off her purple shoes, she'd have none of it, and now her feet rustle the sheets like a dreaming puppy dog. The last thing he thinks before falling asleep is *I should really take off my boots too.*

•••

The ghost of a breeze blows across his face. In the middle of all the brush and trees, the air is starched and a hint of ocean is god-sent. They have to sleep covered in floral camouflage, though, if they care to wake. Another faint wind and some small animal crawls over his toes. He opens his eyes to shoo it away and sees two of the bluest moons focused on him, three inches from his face.

"He scares me," she says. Her shoes touch his shin, as if physical contact will convey what her tiny voice can't.

Butch glances over to see Charlie pacing a small circuit, staring mostly at the covers Sadie hides beneath.

"He slept a whole lot when he was little. He got all his rest then and doesn't need to sleep anymore."

Sadie crimps the sheet under her chin. "Are you scared of him?"

"No. He's my brother. Are you scared of your brother?"

She nods. "He's mean. He tied Gabby to a rocket and shot her into the air."

"That is pretty mean." Butch shapes his face into a picture of empathy. "My brother won't hurt you. And I'll keep you safe from everyone else. I promise."

"Are you scared of anything?" Her lips form the words more than speak them.

Butch tucks her hair behind her ear, snugs the knotted pillow case under her chin.

"No, honey. No, I'm not."

...

Butch again wakes to eyes staring at him, these ones grey like shark skin. By some instinct he doesn't understand, he places his arm over Sadie, snoring beside him.

Charlie is hunched over the foot of the bed, shards of wood around his mouth, a nub of pencil clamped between his teeth. Butch has seen this look before, in the eyes of Charlie's dog when they were little, right before Dad took it to the woods and shot it so the madness wouldn't spread.

"Charlie," Butch says, keeping his voice level. He can feel Charlie's hands trembling. "What're you doing, Charlie?"

Charlie just stares.

"I know you miss her, but it's not Dell, Charlie. It ain't the other girl, neither. Just go take a walk."

"Look at her ears," he says. "Those are my girl's ears. I've held dozens of ears in my hands. I know my daughter's ears."

Butch sits up slowly, doubling the blanket over Sadie, who is beginning to stir.

"Just watch the tree line," Charlie says. "I'll watch her."

Crawling to the edge of the bed, Butch keeps saying, "It's okay, Charlie.

Let's go take a walk. Let's get some air."

Charlie's not having it, though. His teeth click when they finally break through the pencil. He leans forward, stretching his arms out toward Sadie. Butch slips behind him, cinching the crook of his arm against Charlie's throat, bracing his forearm on the back of his neck. His arms burn. He looks down and finds bright red lines, blood dripping from the claw marks.

Easing Charlie's legs to the floor, Butch pulls him toward the door, telling Sadie two times, three times that everything's okay, no one's going to hurt her. He drags his brother outside, pins him against the stucco wall with his forearm.

"Charlie, you with me?" He snaps his fingers in his face a few times. "That is not the girl. Okay? It's not her."

"Just look at her." His words come choked and broken.

"I did, brother. It ain't her." Butch loosens his grip. "That's some poor girl whose momma we killed."

Charlie's nostrils flare when he exhales, tighten when he inhales. His chest rises and falls. After a half-dozen staggered breaths, he nods. Butch releases his grip, inch by inch.

"You look pale," Butch says, opening the door. "I'll buy you some breakfast."

Inside the room, he rousts Sadie from bed, tells her to put on her jacket. "You like eggs?"

She shakes her head.

"Waffles?"

Shakes it again.

"Pancakes, right?"

She smiles and nods. "Blueberry."

"Okay then." Butch shrugs on his jacket and tucks the Mauser inside. When he lays his arm over her shoulders, he can feel the knobs of her bones. "Let's get you a couple inches of pancakes."

Charlie's voice cuts them as they close the door behind them. Butch tightens his grip on Sadie.

"Grey Buick, due north-by-northwest." Charlie motions with his eyes, takes another long drag of his cigarette. Smoke fills the air, his voice. "Saw him over your shoulder a minute ago. He put down his paper and's been sitting there staring since."

"Maybe it's just—"

Concrete chips explode out of the wall behind Butch. The brothers fall to the ground, covering their heads. Charlie's hand flies out by instinct and holds Sadie down. Another round pings against the metal post.

Charlie smacks Butch's hand, points at the corner of the hotel. "Go. I'll cover."

Butch tightens his grip on Sadie's wrist. Her wrist bones rub against one another beneath his fingers. He works his knees beneath him.

Springing to his feet, Charlie cocks the M1911 and shuts his left eye. Exhales, fires, the rear window explodes. Exhales, fires, the driver's door dents a hand's length from the driver, who ducks below the frame. Sadie shrieks when Butch yanks her up and throws her over his shoulder. In a crouched run, he hurries to the corner. The breeze picks up and he thinks he smells burning sugarcane.

Eye still squinting, Charlie lets his breathing become still, a continual loop of inhale and exhale. A trashcan in the corner lays on its side, the newspaper at the lip fluttering in the breeze like palm fronds. A bird's tweet warns about the approaching snake. A dog's bark is the death throes of a peasant. *Come on, you yellow bastard. Just show me your hair.*

"Charlie." Butch's whisper is harsh, as loud as he can make it without shouting. When Charlie doesn't respond he throws a rock a few feet in front of him.

Charlie pops off two shots, shattering the front passenger window and denting the driver's door again. He turns his head, sees his brother sitting on the Harley with the demon-girl in front of him. He checks the Buick again, sees no one, then makes his way to the Indian.

Kicking the engine over, Butch turns, says, "Who the hell was that?"

"A witness," Charlie says.

···

They tuck their bikes two hundred feet back in a cornfield on the outside of town. Sadie says she's hungry. Butch glares at Charlie before he can say anything else.

"Satisfied, Brother?" Charlie throws the lit match to the ground, maybe daring the corn to catch fire.

"That wasn't anything to do with her."

"Sure about that?"

"Sure it wasn't for one of the handful you shot back at the restaurant? Or the couple from Topeka? Or that colored fella in Saint Louis?" Butch steps toward him, getting inside his space. "Hell, how do we know it's not the brother of your CO, trying to right the wrong that grenade couldn't manage to do?"

The cornfield explodes into a rainbow of bright dots. The punch hits his jaw so hard he smells it before he feels it. Dirt scratching the back of his neck, Butch tries to open his eyes only to find Charlie's fist fills the space once, twice, and another in his mouth and on his cheek.

If it wasn't for Sadie's shrieking breaking the blood trance, Charlie might've killed Butch right there in the field.

Charlie pants, propped up over his brother's body. Butch tries to spit but only manages to push the blood over the edge of his mouth, let it drip down his cheek. Their chests rise and fall in unison.

Swinging a leg over, Charlie dismounts, pulls his feet beneath him. He looks down at his brother who is blinking his eyes like he's trying to bat away the sunlight. "We can't go back to that hotel."

Butch's cough is wet. "Everything we got is back there."

Charlie flicks his hands, sending a splattering of red over the dirt and corn stalks. "Guess we need some new stuff."

Sadie sneezes and the brothers startle, turn to her like they'd forgotten she was there.

"You go rustle us up some things," Charlie says, "seeing as how you're the one who got us here. I'll watch the child."

This time Butch manages to spit. A red glob lands on Charlie's boot. "The hell you will."

"Okay. Fine." Charlie rubs his hands in the dirt, giving himself a bath, Infantry Division-style. He stands and looks down at Butch finally hoisting himself on his elbows. Smiling at his brother, he says, "Don't go nowhere."

Then he sinks his boot inside his brother's ribs.

...

Charlie slinks through the aisles of Mason's Hardware, collecting their wares. Incandescent lights strobe above him, turning his skin the colors of a jungle stream: green lichen, then white sun reflection, then the pale blue of a body left in the water. Anyone from the sheriff's department who looked at his collection of items might raise their eyebrow, perhaps tell him to come have a talk. A canvas bag, smaller than the earlier one, plus some rope, bleach, bandanas, window cleaner, rubbing alcohol and a few other assorted items. Charlie's banking on the hillbillies round here to not think twice and just be happy he's giving them some business.

He sets the pile on the counter. The woman at the register examines the pile, looks up at him.

"I'm a geologist."

"A what?" She switches the w and h when she asks.

"I find precious stones and clean them."

She begins to ring up the items, handling each with a suspicious sort of care.

"Sure are some strange tools y'all use."

Charlie ignores her, counting the change in his palm.

"I said, these sure are some strange tools—"

"You ever seen the inside of a human skull?" Charlie shoves his face before hers, not more than an inch between the two. He breathes out of his mouth, letting it wash over her. "Ever heard the sound a brain makes when you sink your fingers in it?"

The woman drops his items with clatter.

Charlie slaps a few bills and some change on the counter. "Put it inside that bag for me." He pauses, considering the bleach and window cleaner. "Second thought, give me a paper bag. Two of them."

He whistles a Hank Williams song while shouldering open the door, a bag held in each arm. When he rounds the corner to his Indian, the sky shatters into a hundred pieces of shrapnel. He feels his jaw click, his tongue squish between his teeth, his ribs shift underneath a boot. Charlie's head bounces off the packed dirt lot. He pushes static from his eyes, blinking away the morning sun.

A man stands above him, a long purple scar that runs from his temple down under his jawline. He kneels down, pressing his knee on Charlie's solar plexus. He relaxes his grip on the barrel of the gun, and Charlie can see a splash of blood on the handle.

The man taps the handle on Charlie's chin.

"We need to come to an understanding."

...

"I'm so hungry I could eat an elephant," Sadie says.

"I'm so hungry I could eat a shark," Butch says.

"You can't eat a shark." She crosses her arms over her chest.

"Not here, you can't. Other places you do."

"An elephant is bigger than a shark."

"Would you rather try to catch a shark or an elephant?"

She taps her finger on her chin. "A bunny."

Butch breathes a laugh. "Sure, it'd be easier to catch a bunny, but you wouldn't want to eat one, would you?"

Her face broadcasts something that could only be called utter revulsion.

"So you're going with the shark, now?"

"But when are we going to eat pancakes? I'm starving." She draws out the *a* for a good ten seconds, running her hand along the stalks for extra emphasis.

"As soon as my brother gets back, we'll get you some waffles."

"I hate waffles!"

"Well it's a good thing you like pancakes." Butch points to the plume of dust snaking through the stalks toward them. "Because we can go eat now."

Sadie dances in circles, clapping her hands like a monkey wearing a fez.

...

Sadie rests one hand on her belly, holds pillow-Gabby in the other. She tries to lean back on the Harley's seat but almost falls off.

"I think I'm going to explode."

"You shouldn't have eaten so much," Butch says.

"You should," Charlie says, handing a bandana and the canvas bag to his brother.

For a flash, Butch wants to react to the jibe, but it'd be half-hearted and he doesn't have the energy. He's focusing on the gas station across the street, running through the motions in his head: the door, the register, the gun, the door. In and out in under a minute.

He watched Charlie standing outside the restaurant the whole time they ate, smoking cigarettes and preparing the supplies. Now, standing in the parking lot of the shuttered Laundromat, neither brother has the concentration nor the will to argue.

Butch pulls Sadie off the bike and deposits her in the alcove of the Laundromat. He points to the boards nailed across the windows.

"See what's in there?"

She kneels down, her thin fingers trying to pry the boards further apart.

"I want you to count how many washing machines and dryers there are. You know how to add, right?"

She nods.

"Count them three times, then add up those numbers and tell it to me. I'll be back before you're done." He hands her a stick and points at the dirt ground. "If you need to write it down, use this."

He pulls his bandana up over his mouth then nods to his brother. They head across the street.

The glass inside the front door shatters when Butch kicks it open. The man bent over a freezer case startles, jumps back. Butch crosses the floor, letting his heels click with each step.

"Money." He cocks the Mauser. "Now."

The man stumbles, and Butch pushes him toward the register. Charlie hangs back by the door, checking outside every few seconds. Dollar bills fall like dead leaves because the man can't steady his hands. A barrel before his eyes doesn't help his composure, so Butch slams the handle on the bridge of his nose. The man howls, drops to the floor. Charlie looks out the door.

Butch slips behind the counter, grabbing fistfuls of dollars and shoving them into the canvas bag. When the register is empty, he heads to the door. Charlie's arm stops him.

"You forgot some." He points at the register.

"It's empty." Butch tries to shove past his brother but can't.

"The ones he dropped." Charlie checks outside again. "Get them."

"It's only a few bucks. We need to go."

Charlie levels his pistol at his brother. "Get them."

The bandana flutters when Butch exhales. He hurries around the counter, crouches and picks up the seven dollars lying on the floor. The man cups his flowing nose, rolling on his back like a bug who can't flip over.

At the door, Butch says, "That good enough for you, Daddy Warbucks?"

Charlie nods and opens the door, motioning for Butch to lead.

Stepping outside, Butch doesn't see Sadie. He starts to run, takes two steps then hears a snap and the world goes black.

Sadie squirms against Edgar's grip, but the man's arms are the kind of thick that proximity to war-time death brings. She kicks her heels against his shins and he gives no reaction, just stares at Charlie, standing over his fallen brother.

Charlie kneels before his brother, reaches out his fingertips and closes his eyes. He whispers a prayer and makes the shape of the cross in the dirt beside him, then stands and faces Edgar.

Edgar finally releases Sadie, pushing her toward Charlie. He holsters his pistol then sinks into his nephew's Buick and turns the engine over. The wheels kick up dust, covering Charlie and Sadie.

She breaks away from Charlie's hand and rushes over to Butch. Her shakes cannot wake him. Her tears cannot roust him. Gabby lies beside her friend. A shadow looms over Sadie. She looks up and the sun is eclipsed by his outline.

"Look here, now," Charlie says. "We need to come to an understanding."

LOLA
ERIC BEETNER

I swear it was never about girls.

"Do you have any idea how much pussy Buddy Holly gets?" my brother asked me.

But I didn't care. Owning a guitar meant I would be in the club. I'd be playing rock and roll, and that's all I planned to play on it. I knew I'd be fighting Mom and Dad the whole way about playing in church, but fuck if I was gonna learn to play "Nearer My God To Thee" when the entire Chuck Berry catalog awaited.

It's like Chuck was talking directly to me when he sang about Johnny B. Goode. I'd have to tell Mom it was her own damn fault for naming me John. I could hear her already. "You were named for the prophet." Well, John can go peddle his gospel someplace else. I got chords to learn.

My major obstacle? No money. But in the true spirit of rock and roll, I didn't let that bother me a whit.

I cased out Covay Music a few times. I nearly drooled over a black and white Fender Stratocaster they had behind the counter. A little out of reach for me, though. I set my sights on a pale blonde Telecaster hung inside the front window. I knew if I could get my paws on that baby I could slide on out the door and be gone in three seconds flat. All I needed was a moment with nobody looking, and I'd have the six strings of my dreams. Some damn fine guitar players used Telecasters. No shame in it.

When I finally took my chance it went like clockwork. There I was, hanging out by the trumpets and other square instruments, leafing through sheet music to look busy. Some pimple-faced kid I recognized from school came out of the back where he'd been taking lessons on the trombone. Thing I never got about music is that if you play a guitar right it seems like a big ol' cock in your hands and you can make it look good. No matter how good you get at the trombone, it still looks like you're jerking off with all that back and forth. Two instruments, each like a dick in your hand—worlds apart.

That's the power of rock and roll.

The kid, Sammy I think his name was, must have not latched his case well enough because when he came out of the back, the case opened up and his disassembled trombone came crashing to the floor sounding like a brass machine gun.

As much as I wanted to hang around and watch the ensuing chaos, I took my chance when I had it and snatched that sweet little lady off the wall and ran like hell.

I named her Lola. Don't know why, she just looked like a Lola.

Now, here's the other thing: I don't play a note. But I got Rock in my blood and it's got to come out somehow. I took Chuck's advice, and I went down by the railroad tracks and sat out under a tree to try out Lola.

She felt sweet as honey in my hands. Every note she sang was like an angel humming on your dick while she sucked you off. I assume.

Yeah, that fifteen minutes with Lola was about the best in my life. Then, as it so often did in my little town, it all went to shit.

...

Pete Guthrie had gathered him up a few friends and they started wearing leather jackets, blue jeans and putting more grease in their hair than it took to run that rusted-out Studebaker they drove around in. Just the fact Pete had a car made him king of the fools he ran with. Most of us got around by screwing wheels from a broken shopping cart to a busted up board and pushing ourselves along by sheer force.

The Guthrie gang thought they were the shit. They thought they were rock and roll. I'd show them.

Only they showed me.

I heard the rumble and smelled burning oil before I saw the car. They rolled to a stop and waited a minute before they turned down the radio. They let Fats Domino finish his song and for a moment there, I thought they might catch me playing on Lola and invite me into the gang, seeing how rock and roll I obviously was.

"Where the fuck did you get that, Johnny?" Pete called out from up on the ridge. He spoke with more of a hick accent than the rest of us, like somehow that would impress people. Guess it worked for his little gang of misfits. Four boys, all in Pete's grade, same as my older brother. All the same greasy-haired shit-for-brains as Pete. I could see them all hanging loose orangutan arms out the windows of the car. Each one of the dipshits had started smoking. I wanted to like hell, but couldn't afford it with my nickel allowance.

"You like it?" I asked. "Pretty, ain't it?"

Pete got out of the car, pinched his cigarette between his thumb and forefinger and shot it skyward. "I asked where the fuck you got it." My invitation to the gang must have been lost in the mail.

"That don't matter," I said.

"Like hell it don't." Pete's gang stepped out of the car and started walking toward me, chugging smoke over their heads. "You ain't got the money for a thing like that."

None of us did is what he meant.

"He can't even play it," said Jerome. He was a kid who could have won a pimple contest. They'd call it in the first round and give him the damn trophy. Weren't no one could beat that kid for size, color, and sheer number of zits on his face.

"I'm learning," I said.

The group reached me. "You didn't answer my question yet," Pete said.

They meant to intimidate, and they did. I was only a freshman and these guys were seniors. Rumor had it they'd been to the city before and bought beer and hard liquor there. One story even said they snatched an old lady's purse and pushed her down, broke her hip and everything. More than one of them was said to have a switchblade knife they got off a Negro man who floated up and down the river selling stuff to people.

I decided to appeal to their outlaw nature. My invite into the gang was sure to follow.

"I stole it."

They laughed. Big time. Like Abbott and Costello. Pete reached down and snatched Lola out of my hands as clean as I lifted her off the wall.

"Then you don't mind if I steal it from you, do you?"

I didn't like the way he pawed over Lola, but there was nothing I could do about it. They all took a moment to comment on her beauty and some of the guys made brown nose comments to Pete about how much he looked like Ritchie Valens or someone. I started to stand, ready for the game to be over and for him to give me my hard-won guitar back, but as soon as I made a move a skinny blond-haired kid who I'd seen at school but didn't know his name whipped his hand out of his pocket and flicked open a switch knife. I stopped in mid get-up and instantly believed all the rumors about the gang. I knew it was better for me to stay put, let Lola go.

"Got something to say?" Blond boy asked. I shook my head. The knife clicked back into itself and went back in his pocket.

Pete and his cronies laughed all the way up the ridge and into their car. Pete tossed Lola to Jerome who took her in the back seat with him. And just like that—she was gone.

...

My brother hated Pete Guthrie, but not as much as I did right then. When I told Mark about it, he made a fist and started punching it into his palm.

"That mother humper," he said.

"I hate him."

"You ought not have stole that guitar, though."

"I know it now." I hung my head in the appropriate amount of shame.

"So what are you gonna do about it?"

"What can I do?"

"Go get your damn guitar back."

"Then bring it back to the store, I guess?"

"Fuck that," Mark said. "We'd never hear the end of it from Pete if that's what we did."

"We?"

"Hey, that douche wad steals from my brother, he steals from me."

So that's how we ended up going after Lola.

...

My brother had no trouble borrowing the pickup truck from Dad, even at night. In their eyes, Mark was a saint. He very nearly could have been, except for his mean streak. The one he got from Dad.

He told me to grab something just in case, and I came to the truck with a baseball bat in hand. Mark looked at it, politely ignored my batting average on the school team, and said, "Good. Yeah, that'll work." Then he hefted Dad's double-ought over his shoulder.

"Jesus H. Christ, Mark. What the hell is that?"

"The only thing Pete is gonna listen to."

He stored it in the gun rack behind the driver's seat, and we lit out of there to go find us a Studebaker.

There weren't more than a few places to hang out in our little town. Most of them centered on the river. As we drove around looking for the gang of idiots, my conviction to the cause of liberating Lola waxed and waned. I'd get all gung-ho about it in my head, and then real quick I'd start to think the whole thing was a bad idea. This was God's way of reminding me thou shalt not steal.

Mark stayed on point. "Piss-ant little punk." I think he enjoyed an excuse to finally let loose on Pete. The primary reason I didn't plead to run home shifted from getting Lola back to wanting like anything to see Pete and his boys brown their trousers when Mark aimed that shotgun their way.

We found them in the cemetery.

If you got over the fact there were dead bodies underneath you, the view overlooking the river was quite nice. The flat, well-groomed piece of land sat high above the riverbank. A popular place in our town, mostly for necking couples, but also for anyone who stole a few beers and wanted a quiet place to drink them. Any adult you talked to would tell stories of how much more inland the graveyard used to be, until the flood of '38. People spoke of the next big flood to be the one to sweep away all the coffins and send them downriver into the next state, making some other river town mighty confused when a few hundred dead bodies show up on their shores boxed and ready for replanting.

I tried looking out over the water to calm myself as we walked out in front of our headlights. I saw the shadows we cast fall over the headstones. Me and Mark, each with a long extension growing from our arms. Mine for sport, his for killing.

"Pete!" Mark called out. "You take my brother's guitar?"

It was a rhetorical question because Pete sat on a thick cut tombstone with Lola slung over his knee. The silver strings gleamed in the headlights from our pickup.

"Your brother's guitar?" Pete said. His voice was full of confidence, not a hint of backing down. He must not have seen the shotgun in the dark. "Last I checked, this here guitar belonged to Covay's."

"You know well and good possession is nine-tenths of the law," Mark said.

"Well, I possess it right now."

"And you got it off a helpless kid." I could have done without the helpless part, but Mark impressed me with his tough guy talk. Like Victor Mature in dirty blue jeans.

"What are you gonna do about it?"

Mark lifted the shotgun and let it rest over his shoulder, butt facing the gang of boys and his finger near the trigger like all he had to do was let it fall forward into blasting position. I copied him with my baseball bat, but I doubt the effect was the same.

I saw the faces on some of the other boys, and they were scared. Pete did a good job of keeping cool.

"You hunting ducks this late at night?"

"No," Mark said. "I'm hunting dicks."

A murmur ran through the gang. People didn't talk back to Pete or his boys. My brother's reputation from school wasn't as a tough guy, either. He'd done the school play last fall and even though he got to kiss Marjorie Popnik, the other boys still called him a fruit for singing and dancing.

Pete stood up, laid Lola down against the tombstone. They moved as a pack toward us. Moths had started to gather in the headlights and cast flickering shadows across the graveyard. Out on the river, lights from the bridge reflected off the water; otherwise, the water was black.

Pete got right in Mark's face. They ignored me, the younger and weaker threat.

"I asked what you're gonna do about it."

Mark had been called out, but I honestly had no idea what the hell he was gonna do. I knew he wouldn't shoot. No way he hated Pete enough to kill him over a stolen guitar. But now he'd been forced into a situation. I had a momentary flash of bravery. I could picture myself swinging my bat at Pete's head like it was a ball on a tee. Maybe if I cracked him hard enough the other guys would split.

Then they'd think twice before stealing from me again.

I didn't get a chance to implement my heroic plan.

Jerome was the first to swing. He planted a fat fist upside Mark's head and the others swarmed like piranhas. Mark threw elbows and his one free hand, but they were all over him in about a second and he was pinned. He tried swinging the shotgun like a club, but couldn't hit anyone. Then I remembered the bat in my hands. Why wasn't I helping? Truth is, I was mesmerized. I'd never seen a brawl this close before.

No one paid me a lick of mind as they set to beating Mark. They didn't make much noise. A lot of grunts and the squeaking sound of leather jackets getting a workout. The whole act was lit up by the pickup truck. The sudden disturbance in the air around us sent the moths flying in crazy circles. Dust from a fresh grave kicked up under their feet as the gang took their shots at my brother.

Then the shotgun went off.

Good Christ, I'd never heard anything louder. Everyone stopped. Jerome flew back grabbing at the side of his head. He screeched in pain, and the echo came back across the water a few seconds later.

As he bent over in the headlamp beam, I saw him take his hand away from his ear and watched as a spill of blood drooled out over the graves.

"He fucking shot me!"

Everyone released the breath they'd been holding, seeing proof he wasn't dead. Then Pete and the gang turned to Mark who stared in horror at Jerome and the bright red splotch where his ear used to be.

"You fucking shot him," Pete said as if anyone in the tri-county area couldn't hear Jerome's loud yell.

Mark dropped the shotgun. I could see in his face it was partly an act of surrender and partly because he didn't want another accident. He knew he wouldn't get so lucky twice.

The four remaining boys all reached to grab him at the same time. It made the beating he was getting before seem like playground time. The short-cropped blond in the leather jacket grabbed the bat out of my hand, stuck the small end into my gut and then raised it to Mark.

I didn't see him get hit the first time. I was already on my way to the ground. From the cool grass I watched them drag Mark away toward the river.

By the time I got my breath back they had disappeared over the rise. I dragged myself up and stumbled forward through the rows of headstones toward the water. I left Jerome behind, screaming as he crouched over, tripping between stone crosses and carved granite. I passed Lola on the way and resented her for ever getting me mixed up in this. It was easier to blame someone else.

Still ten rows of grave markers from the riverbank and the headlights ran out of beam to light the rest of the way. I followed the sounds of my brother's beating.

The drop down from the graveyard to the muddy riverbank was a good ten feet. I felt pretty confident Mark had been thrown down. I slid on my backside and ended up a few yards from where all four boys formed a circle around my brother as they threw punches and kicks. Pete took hold of the baseball bat and brought it down over and over onto the dark shape I knew was Mark.

"Stop it," I said. I don't think I'd ever heard a weaker noise. The frogs on the bank sounded tougher. I could do nothing but sit by and wait for it to end. Whether they were tired or they felt they'd done enough, it ended soon.

One by one the boys passed me, heaving breaths as they grabbed hold of tree roots and climbed their way back to the cemetery. Only after the last of them had gone did I run to Mark.

•••

Mark spent five days in the hospital. His face looked all puffed up like a dead fish on the shore after a few hot days. His right eye didn't look good at all. Several ribs were broken, but that was no shock the way they kicked at him. And that dumb baseball bat I brought? I blamed that for his broken jaw.

I played dumb with Mom and Dad, and I think their patience with me was growing short. Mom read several passages from the Bible about lying, hoping I'd get the hint.

I had bigger things on my mind. Things like Pete Guthrie and how to fuck that boy up.

I spent those five days with my brain boiling away on a hot plate of rage. Not just at Pete and the boys, but at myself for being useless as tits on a hammer. A goddamn disgrace, that's what I was. Standing by like a cigar store Injun while my brother got his brains beat out.

Mom rubbed her fingers raw on the edges of the cross she hung around her neck, praying for a miracle. Some good it did. Before the doctors finally let Mark come home, they pulled Mom and Dad aside and told them the eye didn't make it. It'd be a good two months before a glass one would come in, too.

So my brother came home, one eyeball and three teeth lighter and with a kind of haze around him like he was always only half awake.

Time to right my wrong. For Mark and Lola.

•••

It only took a little asking around to get Pete's address. Way the hell out in the country. No wonder he needed a car. If I showed up there with my baseball bat again, I'd get beat this time. I needed something more.

I waited for nightfall, then slid open my bedroom window and dropped down to the mossy rocks beneath. I wasn't the saint Mark was, and I was younger, so Mom and Dad would have said no to me going out that late. With them sitting up and reading Bible passages to my brother while he stared at nothing, it was easy to come and go as I pleased.

I biked downtown and leaned my Schwinn up against a lamppost outside Humbert's Department Store. A light breeze blew the brand new traffic light on its wire hanging over the intersection. A waste of money, if you ask me, because there sure weren't any cars around.

I walked down the length of the big picture window at Humbert's, past the baseball gloves and the horseshoe sets. Down to the end where three pistols lay all in a row next to a rifle, a pair of waders, and a stuffed mallard duck.

I took one last look around, then pictured Mark's face and his empty eye socket. It was all the courage I needed—hell, I'd already stolen something much bigger.

I punched my fist through the glass and grabbed the closest pistol and the box of ammo next to it. It made a hell of a racket, but no one was around to care. I tried to keep my sleeve up over my arm but I still caught a pretty good dagger of glass across the back of my hand. Back on my bike, it got so I was bleeding real good and had to wrap my hand with the bandana I always kept in my back pocket.

It was a hell of a long ride. The pavement ran out when I still had two miles or more to go. I stood up on my pedals and kept my head down into the wind kicking up. I could feel mud spatter the back of my jacket from my back tire digging through the ruts in the country road.

Every time my bravery started to waiver I thought of Mark's bruised face and missing eye. Then I thought of Lola. If I got her back, I was gonna walk right into Mark's room and give her up as a present. He'd let me borrow her. We could both learn and start a band and be done with this shitball town.

Finally I saw it. A weak light hung over a sagging porch. Overgrown farm land spread out on either side of the unstable looking house. The wind blew any clouds away and the three-quarters moon lit the land well. I didn't see or smell any livestock.

I let my bike fall at the turn off into their long driveway. I put a hand on the gun in my pocket. I remembered then I had to load the thing. It took me a while, figuring how to crack the barrel of the revolver, lining up the tiny bullets in the moonlight all while working with a lumpy, bandana-wrapped hand. I got all six shots in and closed it up with a heavy metal click. I hadn't heard a sound like it before.

I convinced myself Dad would be proud. Not of the stealing—that's a sin. But of defending my brother. I'd left out Pete's name from my retelling of the story. I figured it was Mark's place to I.D. his attackers. Playing dumb is what Mom and Dad expected of me, so I played into their hand.

Dad wouldn't have had the guts to come out here. Even for his own boy.

Well, his youngest was about to become a man.

...

I knocked on the door with the butt of the gun. I had no plans to shoot anyone. I was going to get Lola back and prove to Pete he couldn't push around our family and get away with it. I hoped like hell I could make him piss his pants thinking I'd come to do him in. But that seemed like wishful thinking.

The door eased open, and I found myself looking at a boy a few years younger and several inches shorter than myself. His shirt was dirty, so was his face. He wore no pants and his little bald dick bobbed like a fishing lure. His eyes were red and snot ran out of his nose into his mouth, but he didn't care.

Neither of us said a word.

I remembered the gun in my hand and put it down at my side.

"What the fuck, Gordy? Where you at?" Pete's voice traveled from another room. For the first time I looked over Gordy's shoulder and into the house.

It was filthy. And there was a man passed out on the living room floor. A big man with a balding head, face down on the wood planks. He wore blue jeans over a threadbare union suit. In one hand was an empty bottle of whiskey and in the other, still clenched in a tight fist despite his being out like a light, was a belt.

Gordy followed my gaze and turned his body to look at the man. When he turned he showed me his backside, red as raspberries in summer, crisscrossed with marks. Things started to make a whole lot of sense.

"Gordy, I said, 'What the fuck?'"

Pete came into the room from a hallway holding a shotgun in one hand. A Pre-War single barrel, worn wood stock, rust spots around the sight and the hammer. I wondered if it would still shoot. He stopped when he saw his little brother at the door and me there on the porch. Pete had also been crying. His shirt was off and I saw the same red marks slashed across his chest. He wiped at his nose with the back of his hand.

"The fuck you doing here?"

I'd almost forgotten myself. I lifted the gun, stepped over the threshold.

"I want my guitar back."

Gordy sniffed a wad of snot deep into his head. Pete stared at me, at the gun outstretched in my hand. His shotgun stayed aimed at the floor.

"That fuckin' guitar," he said under his breath, shaking his head and staring at the ground. He lifted his eyes to mine. "It true your brother lost an eye?"

"It's true."

"Shit." Pete looked genuinely regretful for a moment. "Jerome's ear is pretty much gone too. 'Least Mark can get a glass eye. Jerome's got a hunk of torn meat on the side of his head for the rest of his life."

Pete moved nervously. He turned so I could see part of his back and I could tell the red marks were worse there. I slowly realized he hadn't carried the shotgun into the room because he heard a knock at the door. He hadn't known I was there. He brought that gun in for another purpose.

"Is that your Daddy?" I said, pointing to the man on the ground with the barrel of my pistol.

"Yeah," Pete said. "That's the son-of-a-bitch." He spat on the floor near his Dad's unconscious head.

I turned to Gordy, my Christian charity getting the better of me. "He do that to you?"

Gordy stared back at me with as much understanding as a pig in a schoolroom.

"He don't talk," Pete said.

As he stood there, Gordy began to piss. He acted like he didn't even know he was doing it, letting it fly all over the floorboards.

"God dammit, Gordy," Pete scolded.

I got a feeling I'd walked in on a scene played out a thousand times in this tiny room. Dad, dead drunk and needing to hit someone. Mom, long gone to the grave or the next state. Only targets left were the boys. Dad would pass out, Pete would get the gun, think about it. Wish he could pull the trigger. Then back up to the gun rack it would go to gather more rust.

But Pete and Gordy's problems were not my own. I tightened my grip on the gun, the bandana around my hand moist with blood.

"You got my guitar or what?"

"Why don't you get the hell out of here? This ain't your house. You can't bust up in here and start giving orders."

"All I want is my guitar."

"Or what?" Pete stared at me with eyes hard as nails.

"Or I'll shoot." Even I wasn't convinced.

"Bullshit. You ain't gonna shoot nobody."

My hand started to shake. "Like hell I ain't."

Pete looked from the tip of my gun barrel down to his Dad, the slow breath of the unconscious man lifting his chest in a steady rhythm.

"Well, what if you did shoot someone?" Pete looked down at his Dad again. I watched his face. He was trying to tell me something. The fresh piss smell hung between us as he started to get nervous on his feet.

"Just give me back my guitar."

"I will," Pete said. He licked his lips, swallowed hard. "You do something for me first."

I followed his eyes. I could read between his lines. He wanted me to shoot his old man.

"No, Pete."

"Why not? You said you was gonna hurt somebody, didn't you? You came out here to get your guitar back. Maybe give me a little 'what for' because of your brother."

"You beat his eye right out of his head. And he ain't right no more. He ain't right." I stifled tears, forced them down and my voice to calm.

"I know all about not bein' right." Pete looked to his piss-stained brother. He lifted the shotgun and pointed it at my face. My gun shrank in the presence of the long barrel, the black eye staring me down. "You're gonna do it," he said.

I shook my head.

"You'll do it," he said again, tightening his grip around the stock of the gun, his thin muscles tensing up and down his arm.

"No."

"You want your guitar back, don't you? You want to get back for your brother, right?"

"I can't do it, Pete." I took a few steps back toward the door.

"Do it, Johnny. Do it, big burglar man." He moved closer, the barrel practically breathing on me now. "Do the old son-of-a-bitch. He deserves it." Pete began to cry. No sound came out, no choking sobs interrupted his angry commands. Only the full tears dripping from his eyes gave any indication. His words began to turn from military-style orders to pleading.

"Do it, Johnny. Go on. He's the one who stole your guitar. It's his blood that runs in me. His blood that made me do it. He's the one. He's the bad one."

I couldn't stand the weakness in his voice. His pleas came faster, more tear-stained.

"No," I shouted. "Why don't you do it?"

Pete froze. A tear hung in his eyelashes, unwilling to drop now that his whole body had gone to steel. The steady wheeze of his Dad filled the quiet around us. I watched Pete's eyes go bloodshot in front of me.

He whipped the shotgun away from my face, swung it down to the floor in one motion and fired.

My body jumped involuntarily, but I tried to keep as still as I could.

He'd caught his Dad in the back of the head. He fired again. Everything above the old man's shoulders was gone, replaced by a smear of blood and a hole in the wood planks of the floor.

Behind me, Gordy sniffed up another ball of snot. A thin line of piss ran down a ridge in the floorboards seeking low ground as it mixed with the blood spread out around the body.

Pete didn't move. He stared down at his Dad, his face as blank as his brother's. He let the shotgun droop in his hands.

I don't know what it was, maybe the weird look in Pete's eye before he turned away, but I understood him. Understood why he did it. The dumb, pantsless kid behind me and the leaning shitbox of a house made me feel sorry for him more than the beatings. I walked past him, down the hall I'd seen him come out of, and found Lola in the room he obviously shared with Gordy.

Back in the main room, both brothers stared at the body of their father, unmoved on the floor. The bottle in his grip unbroken, his head in shattered pieces.

Lola felt cold in my hands. She didn't feel right anymore. I leaned her up against the arm of the couch and said, "You keep it." She was nothing but trouble, and this house was where trouble lived.

I stepped out the door without another word.

I slid the gun into my pocket, remembering a bridge I'd passed over on my ride out there where I could dump the thing into a small river.

As I rode home I hummed to myself. *Rock and Roll is here to stay. It will never die.*

Fuck, those guys got it all wrong. Everything dies someday.

BLUE JEANS AND A BOY'S SHIRT
CHAD EAGLETON

The '49 Ford skidded around the sharp curve, shooting suddenly out of the mountain fog into clear night. On the straightaway, Lonnie Bonner laid the hammer down. The big beast ate blacktop with an engine rumble, thundering for the high concrete spanning 300 feet of coastal drop when the headlights hit a girl crossing the bridge. The high beams pulled her out of the darkness, a thin figure in blue jeans and a boy's shirt, dark hair trailing down her back and swaying with her walk and the wind.

Lonnie ground the gears downshifting and stomped the brakes. Uncle Luther's sawed-off flew off the front seat into the floorboard. The girl turned at the loud screech of metal on metal, framing herself between the lights to stare back at the dark windshield as Lonnie jerked the Ford into the left lane. The coupe grazed the guardrail, shooting sparks as it lurched to a loud stop.

For a moment, Lonnie didn't know where he was or what had happened. He had been fine coming out of LA until the Santa Lucia Mountains rose out of the sea and night fell. The falling brought fog and twisted his thoughts, sending him deep inside his head and spiraling through memories of the war.

He breathed deep and loud, hands squeezing the wheel, forearms taut and back straight. The girl on the bridge brushed a long strand of hair from her face. Lonnie rubbed his eyes to see if she was real—after the war, he wasn't sure what was and what wasn't. When he opened them, she was walking again, moving without a word.

That made him mad. He needed an apology, some acknowledgement that he was there and that he mattered. If he couldn't get one, he'd settle for fear—a quickened pace across the bridge, darting onto the shoulder and up the mountain.

Lonnie grabbed his cigarettes off the dash and quickly lit one. He wrapped the shotgun in his blue windbreaker and tossed it in the back. He released the brake and hit the gas.

He cruised up behind her, and the girl kept walking.

Lonnie tightened his jaw, clamped down on his smoke, and pressed harder on the accelerator. Too hard. The Ford shot forward and he nearly hit her again. He braked, then eased way off the gas.

Ain't gonna turn, he thought.

When she didn't, he flicked ash out the window hard enough to lose the cherry. He bit down on the dead cigarette and honked his horn. The noise startled her. He saw it, the shoulder jerk and the stutter step, but she kept moving across the bridge.

Walking. Always walking. Like she was afraid to stop.

Lonnie swerved to the other lane and matched her pace. One-handing the wheel, he leaned over, yelling out the open window, "What the hell you doing?"

The girl lowered her head, staring at her Keds or maybe the road as the wind lashed lengths of dark hair across her face. Lonnie repeated himself, started to honk again, and she looked straight at him. "What the fuck are *you* doing?"

His shock sent the Ford weaving between rail and line. He had wanted her to say something but didn't expect her to. Steadying the wheel and not knowing what else to do, he said, "Driving."

She nodded and kept walking.

Lonnie checked for oncoming traffic. The road was quiet, dark, and empty. When he looked back at her, the girl was veering sharply toward the car. Again, he punished the brakes, forcing the coupe to a loud halt.

She leaned in the passenger window. "I'm walking, so give me a ride," she said, brushing her hair behind her ears and resting her chin on her hands. "Just back home. It's not far."

He eased back in his seat. Remembering the cigarette in his mouth, he relit it and mumbled, "Yeah?"

"Yeah," she said. "Not far at all."

The ocean wind swept over the bridge and whipped the girl's hair. She tilted her head from the gust until she seemed to be looking somewhere else. If her bright eyes weren't liars, somewhere else was far away and much better than there.

Lonnie liked that. The way her eyes looked. He couldn't see her face very well in the dim interior, but her eyes seemed so beautiful and so sad, he had to turn away to check the road again, knowing there was nothing but trees and darkness and shadows. That deep emptiness he now saw everywhere.

"My parents have a cabin up here." The wind calmed. "Turnoff is just about ten miles back."

Lonnie flicked his cigarette off the bridge. "I almost killed you."

"You didn't," she said.

"But I almost—"

"You didn't."

"Girls shouldn't walk the highway alone."

"That's why you should give me a ride. I've been out here too long. My father is probably worried."

Lonnie looked back at her. Her eyes were barely visible in the messy curtain of hair, but the arch of her lip cut through the black with sharp curves. "And you shouldn't ride with strangers," he said.

"There are worse people on the road."

"How do you know?"

She shrugged. "You got a red light?"

"No."

"Rope?"

"Nope."

"A knife?"

He shook his head.

She shrugged again. "Nothing to worry about."

I've got a gun, he thought. *That's something, isn't it?* He didn't know and wasn't sure he wanted to. The only answers he ever got were ones he didn't like. "Ah'right, get in."

She slid into the seat and slammed the door closed with both hands. Lonnie drove forward onto the shoulder. As he turned the coupe around and slowly headed back over the bridge, memories amassed in the night behind his eyes, waiting for ambush on the other side of the fog. When the first wheels hit the concrete, his heart began to beat faster and faster. Each beat squeezed his chest tight and tighter, constricting his lungs and shallowing his breath. The closer to the fog, the more each and every labored inhale narrowed his vision, drawing him back to places he did not wish to return.

The girl didn't notice.

Hoping to stay with her in the car, Lonnie licked his dry lips, then said,

"What are you doing out here?"

"Told you," she said. "Walking."

"To where?"

"Nowhere in particular."

"Late at night? On a bridge in the middle of nowhere? I heard motor-cycles earlier." The bikes had been worse than the fog. The loud rumble of their engines echoed through the mountains like a barrage of big guns unleashing hell, a sound that often filled his dreams.

"So? I saw them. They're just biker trash." She shrugged, pulled her feet up onto the seat, and faced her door. She looked fragile staring out the window in her boy's checkered shirt. Lonnie found it sad and comforting, but both feelings depressed him.

"What are *you* doing driving around this late like a creep?" she asked.

The coupe hit the fog. He hid his nervous breath with a smoky exhale. "How old are you?"

"Younger than you, but old enough," she said, smiling at shadows.

"You should be more careful."

Lonnie tried focusing on her voice, reminding himself as she spoke, that she was here, now, with him. "*You* should be more careful. You're the one who almost hit *me*," she said. "What's your name?"

"Lonnie," he said. "Lonnie Bonner."

"Lonnie Bonner." She nodded. "Are *you* what they call a hood? Keep straight."

"What?"

She gathered her hair in her hands, pulled it loosely back over her shoulders and twisted in the seat to face him. "Are you what they call a hood?"

He lit a cigarette. "What's a hood?"

"A hoodlum, I think. A juvenile delinquent, I guess."

"I look like a kid?"

"No."

"You?"

"Do I look like a kid?" She laughed. "What do you call a female hood? A hoodress?"

"No, what's your name?"

"Daisy." She stretched her legs along the seat. Her jeans were cuffed high, nearly to her calves. Her legs were nice. Not as tan as he'd thought, but nice except for the scratches on her ankles, like she had run through low brush.

The coupe veered toward the wooded shoulder. Lonnie straightened the wheel and said, "Nice to meet you, Daisy."

"I don't like my name." She leaned her head back against the passenger door and the wind snatched her hair, snapping it out the open window like a hot rodder's foxtail. "My father named me after a character in *The Great Gatsby* by F. Scott Fitzgerald. I used to think that was sweet and special. Then I read the book—I don't wanna be shallow."

"You go to college?" Lonnie thought she sounded college.

"For a semester. Keep going straight. Follow the road." She paused in her story to run her tongue across her top teeth and peek through the windshield. "Have you read it?"

Lonnie shook his head. He had read a lot before the war—mostly comic books and pulp magazines. Once back stateside, he hadn't tackled anything other than the headlines on the daily paper, and then only rarely. He told her it could have been worse. "Coulda named you after the Duck."

"What? Oh, ha ha." She cocked her head against the seat. Lonnie glanced at her to stay anchored in the moment. He turned away when he saw the angle of her neck, the swathe of shadows across her face like the raw tread marks of a tank.

"Where you from, Lonnie Bonner?"

"Kentucky."

"Why drive all the way out here?" She raised her head and pointed. "Keep straight by hanging slightly left. That's not a road road."

He did and said, "Just because."

"Long drive just because."

"Thought you meant up here." Lonnie shook his head. "I live in Los Angeles now. The City of Angels."

She crinkled her eyes, cocked her chin, and stared at him like she was trying to place something. "No one says that 'cept on TV."

He nodded, shrugged—he'd never seen one anyway. "Nothing for me back home."

"What do you do?"

"You mean for money?"

"Yeah."

"What do you do?"

She closed her eyes. "Nothing. I'm a girl. They tell me I'm waiting to get married. That's why only one semester of college. My father pulled me out. My parents tell me I failed, but I got mostly A's." She paused with her lips open like there was something else she wanted to say but she wasn't sure if she should. Lonnie started to speak, but her words escaped, "Everyone tells me what to do, and none of it makes sense."

He nodded.

After the war, Old Man Turner had offered him a sales job at his Pine Knot store. Lonnie didn't have much use for appliances and didn't want to sell them, never particularly wanted to sell anything really, but everyone kept telling him to take the offer and he didn't get it. He could have worked a job he hated without going into the Army, and he could have been miserable without shedding another man's blood.

But, he figured, what do I know?

Turner thought a medal winner would draw more business, and it did. When Lonnie started, his shifts were packed. Mostly with single women. Korea raised him up in their eager eyes, from ridge runner with greasy hair and big teeth to fight-worthy marriage option. But men showed up too. They wanted to shoot the shit at the counter or trade lunch for a war story they'd later steal for their own. Though one fella Lonnie knew back in school and never much cared for was the most upfront. Not bothering with the pretense of shopping, he explained, "Expect you're gonna get a lot of tail thrown your way. I'll take what doesn't stick."

Thankfully, the job didn't last long. After only a couple weeks, everyone finally realized Lonnie was a shit salesman. The people who were going to buy something from him had, and those purchases were only for their perceived added value. "See this washer? You know who sold me this washer? A goddamned medal winner."

Daisy pulled her legs up and twisted against the seat. "You a detective? There've been detectives here before looking for people. Up here, everyone is hiding from something."

"*77 Sunset Strip*? You like that show?" He tossed his cigarette. "I'm not a detective. Never been to La Cienega Boulevard and Alta Loma Road, and you can't have my comb. Wouldn't want it anyway. The pomade pools along the spine."

"I know someone who can get you a job parking cars at Dino's."

"I drive a truck," he said. "Delivery."

"That's a lot of driving. You must like it."

"I do." Before that night, driving was the only time his mind quieted. Lonnie understood being behind the wheel. It made sense to him like nothing else ever did. Now that was gone too. "You?"

"Can't drive," she said. "Don't know how to pump gas either."

"Can you not? That why you're walking?"

She was quiet for a long minute, then, "Yup."

"Cause they're making you wait, right?"

"Yeah, for a husband." She snorted. "Did you read *On The Road*?"

The coupe hit a sloppy S-curve. Lonnie braked and downshifted, moving fast but controlled. On the inside swing, headlights broke through the thick wood rising up the mountainside. The trees magnified the loud rumble of motorcycles and—

East of the Chorwon Valley, night fell hours ago. Reinforcing Outpost Harry after last night's slaughter, they're too far from the main line for supportive fire, trying to hold the bunkers and the trenches against heavy artillery, constant mortaring, and suicide raids. Chinese won't stop. Big guns and bombs blast and blast. He's afraid he's going to go deaf and blind.

The big boy from Brooklyn with the last name no one can say thumps his arm for a smoke.

Lonnie hands him one.

Brooklyn says, "Haros."

"What?"

"S'what the Greeks call Harry." Fire-flash across the sky. "He takes you to the underworld."

A single access road sweeps around the back of the outpost. Before the light dies, Lonnie sees all those other eyes in the dark. Enemy troops crawl up the hillside, scramble over trenches.

"These are his teeth," Brooklyn says before his throat opens with a pop that sounds like cheap fireworks.

Lonnie raises his rifle. Brooklyn sprays red. Wet and screaming, Lonnie pulls the trigger—crack, crack, crack. Shoot. Move. Shoot. Move. Don't think just shoot and move the rifle. These aren't people. Just shoot—

Daisy smacked his arm.

Headlights flooded the back windshield, bobbed like will-o-the-wisps in the rearview. Lonnie made five bikes coming up fast.

Quick breath. Focus. Left hand, wheel. Be here. Right hand, gear shift. You're in the car. "They friends of yours?"

"I don't have any friends," Daisy said without pity.

"Yeah, me neither."

The bikes spread across the road behind them and revved their engines in a deep, warning growl.

"They're showing off," he said. "Don't worry."

The middle rider broke suddenly from the pack, swooped around the coupe's right rear fender, and cruised alongside Daisy's window.

Lonnie pulled her to the middle of the seat.

The rider shook his head and cackled, then gunned his engine and raced ahead. Lonnie made his ride for a '55 Triumph Trophy. "They'll follow," he said.

He watched Daisy's eyes scan the windows like a creature feature ingénue. She breathed ragged, grabbed his bicep. "Lonnie—"

The Triumph blocked the middle of the road ahead.

"Shit!" Lonnie crushed the brakes. The big Ford screamed. He felt Daisy come off the seat and grabbed her tight, pulling her into his lap as he swerved, fighting the change in momentum and struggling one-handed for control.

The coupe careened to a stop, nearly smacking the Triumph with its heavy rear end.

The rider didn't care. He dropped one foot onto the road and spun his bike in circles until the tires burned and smoked.

"You okay?"

Daisy didn't answer.

The rider howled, circled his bike a final time, and then disappeared into the next bank of fog and darkness.

Behind them, another biker burst from the far side of the line. He swept wide across the highway and charged.

"He's going to hit us!"

"No," Lonnie said.

The second biker leaned down low over his bike to cut resistance. Lonnie felt Daisy tremble. He gritted his teeth, watched and waited.

The biker gathered more speed.

Lonnie felt the muscle in his jaw tighten and bulge.

The biker swerved and kicked the door as he roared past.

The kick was cue. The gang gunned for the Ford, weaving across the road and cutting in front of each other before splitting sides to circle the coupe.

Daisy screamed.

Something hit the back window.

Another boot thudded against Lonnie's door.

A fist banged on the roof.

A dirty face spat in the window.

A pipe cracked the back windshield.

Lonnie's rage pushed him past red. His directionless and unspecified anger gathered shape and focus again. "Get down," he growled.

Daisy hunkered down in the floorboard, ducking and covering like Bert the Turtle.

The motorcycles broke their circle and followed the Triumph's route to the next fog bank.

Lonnie cursed and quickly turned the coupe around, barking "How far?"

But the Triumph had been waiting. As soon as the gang hit the fog, he shot out, passing his fellow riders in a blur and hurtling toward the coupe.

"What?" Daisy asked softly.

The rider rode low and fast.

Lonnie shifted and revved the Ford in response. "To your house. How far?"

"Close."

"Don't let me pass it," Lonnie said and hammered the gas.

The Ford rocketed down the road. Daisy hit her head against the dash. She umpfed and covered up tighter.

"Come on you, mother!" Lonnie shifted gears and tried to push the accelerator through the floor.

The motorcycle didn't waiver. It flew toward them head-on.

"Fuck you!" The Ford growled and devoured roadway, ready to smash the motorbike.

At the last minute, the Triumph veered hard right. The handlebars grazed the coupe's side-mirror. The bike wobbled. For a second, Lonnie thought he was going to lay it down but the rider regained control and slid his back wheel to a swinging stop, then raised one arm and wolf-whistled.

The gang streaked out of the fog bank, yelling as they again raced past the Ford.

"Goddamnit!" Lonnie hit the brakes and cranked the wheel, taking the coupe into a power slide. He shifted before it had even come to a full stop, moving his feet, charging the engine, ready to pursue.

Then, from the floorboards, a quiet and frightened noise as the line of taillights retreated into the gloom.

Daisy touched his knee and looked up at him.

Lonnie Bonner had never been what he thought of as religious. While his family had made him attend church every Sunday, it was just a thing. Something you did. How you hedged your bets—"I may fuck this life up, but the next one's covered." Seeing Daisy's face, he wondered then, again, as he did often, if the war had cost him something that marked his place in the world. Stolen something that would keep him forever apart.

Lonnie broke her look before tears came. He drove slowly forward and turned around. He checked the rearview once, then reached down and said, "You okay?"

She nodded.

He helped her into the seat, then lit a cigarette and drove away in silence, thinking only about death and hoping that when it came, it too was quiet and empty. Maybe then this loneliness wouldn't be so bad, it was just practice.

...

Lonnie turned the radio on a quarter mile from the showdown. He hoped the music would cover the pounding of his heart and hide his attempts to breathe through the return of his low and abiding panic. It did, but not much else. The guitar and upright bass coming through the speakers offered no solace. The only nice moments were when Daisy sang along to the radio. Her voice was soft and high, pretty but slightly off tune to Gene Vincent's pleading or Buddy Holly's hiccough.

Mostly, he drove with Daisy curled up in the seat, face pressed against the rolled-up window. He drove, trying to focus on the rhythm between brake and gearshift, wheel and accelerator. He drove, hoping to lose himself in the pavement's sweep and curve. He drove like he could outrun everything but knowing he could outrun nothing.

He drove like Daisy had walked. Afraid to stop.

When the tree line broke and the fog brooded somewhere far behind, Daisy kicked her feet off the seat, slapped the dash and pointed, "Turn here. No, here. Right here."

Lonnie pulled over onto the shoulder, following her finger onto a rocky path that hugged the cliffside and trailed down toward the ocean. "You live down there? By the water?"

She didn't answer.

The Ford bounced over the ruts, and Daisy slid to the edge of her seat, all ten fingers resting on the dash as she stared ahead. Lonnie wanted to turn around and head back up to the coastal highway, but her route gave him no choice but forward.

"You said your father would be worried."

"He's not there."

"How do you know?"

The headlights revealed only a few more yards of path and the dark hint of beach. "He's never been there. Not once. He bought it sight unseen. It belongs to his ex-wife now. She comes up here to get away with her daughter, but really to have crazy parties and fuck boys fresh off the bus. She has a diaphragm and lets them finish inside her. She's had the clap twice. Like if she falls far enough, dad'll come back around to catch her." Daisy closed her eyes and shook her head.

Lonnie stopped the coupe at the start of the long and narrow beach. Down there by the ocean, without the shade of the mountains and the trees or the fog, the night was bright and lit by a moon round enough that it couldn't be called anything but full.

Daisy patted his leg. "Drive," she said.

For the first time, he saw her clearly in the light. Away from the gloom and the tyranny of his thoughts, she looked prettier than he imagined. The shape of her face, the curve of her cheekbones, the sweep of her mouth, the set of her eyes all looked perfect to him. Perfect except for the dark places he now saw were bruises.

"Go. Please." She grabbed the door handle and slapped the dash.

Lonnie swallowed, then did as she said. Driving forward, he felt the Ford sink a little into the beach and slow to a crawl. He pressed harder on the gas. The tires spun for a moment, flung sand, then rolled forward.

He stopped the coupe midway between cliff and sea, leaned back with one hand across the front seat. He could see it now. The ocean looked like a single moving dark line. Daisy held the door handle like she was waiting for permission. When he reached out and brushed her shoulder, she opened her door and sprinted down the beach, disappearing quickly beyond the headlights' glow. The battering surf swallowed the sound of her Keds in the wet sand and left him alone in the car, in the dark, with all the faces.

...

It wouldn't be that bad would it?

Lonnie lit a cigarette and unwrapped the shotgun. Strange thoughts occurred to him then. If he blew his brains out, would his lost chances fly from his shattered skull like a coop of loosed birds? Could Daisy pluck them from the air? Swallow them whole before they disappeared west of where ocean met sky?

Lonnie placed the barrel under his chin and closed his eyes. The dead readied for roll call. He walked the line in his private dark, counting their faces and measuring their sorrow.

Brooklyn waited front and center. His friend's face came to him the most in the hours and hours before sleep, when drink carried him beyond forget and straight to misery. The New Yorker has been Lonnie's only real friend ever. Growing up he had had buddies. Kids he played with. Boys and girls from class. A few lasted through high school. One even wrote him twice when he was overseas. But Brooklyn was different.

And Brooklyn was dead. Stolen with a bullet.

Lonnie opened his eyes and looked down. He watched his hand move to the trigger. He hooked the deadly comma with his thumb.

If it hurts, it'll only be a second. Make a hell of a mess—he pushed gently on the trigger, watched the hammer slowly rise—*and Daisy will find it.*

His thumb froze. The hammer waited. He imagined her walking to the car, opening the door and seeing him there. His mouth open and slack. His shattered skull still smoking. Blood and brains dripping from the hardtop. He heard her cry out and watched himself swim behind her eyes to wait forever and ever.

Lonnie screamed. He released the trigger and tossed the shotgun. He beat the wheel with his fists, then squeezed it like a neck and gasped soundlessly for longer than he knew.

When he found his breath, he looked back at the beach, thought he saw someone moving out there and for a moment, again, he wasn't afraid.

He dried his face with the bandana from his back pocket, then smoothed his hair. He killed the lights and followed Daisy's wild footprints down to the ocean.

•••

Her boy's shirt billowing in the wind, Daisy waded out in the water with her jeans rolled up to her knees. The rough waves slapped her legs mid-calf as she watched the distant and endless horizon.

"Daisy!" he yelled over the surf.

She swayed with the smaller waves and ran from the bigger ones like she was both eager and afraid of shore and sea.

Lonnie lit a cigarette, inhaled deep, and held it until his lungs burned.

"I thought you left me!"

"No," he said too quietly for her to hear.

"Ever been to the beach before, Lonnie Bonner from Kentucky?"

"Not this one," he said.

She walked high through the waves. As she approached, the wind mangled her hair, turning her into a faceless thing, a small voice through a damp curtain of black. "I like the beach, especially when it's like this. It's the only time I'm not thinking about something."

Lonnie took a step, stopping at the line of damp sand where she had kicked off her Keds. Once on shore, Daisy slipped her wet feet into her shoes and reached her hand out toward him as if to touch his hair. He saw the light from the moon catch his slick and reflect in her eyes. Her hair stilled suddenly, the wind dying as the waves slowed to a gentle and drowsy slap. "If your hair wasn't so greasy," she said, "you'd look a little like James Dean."

He smiled, knowing he looked nothing like James Dean.

"He died the day my parents' divorce was finalized."

Lonnie nodded, trying not to stare at the bruises. *What happened to you?*

Daisy turned once more to the ocean. He watched her looking—liked looking at her looking—and wondered what she saw and hoped it was different than the things he saw out there, moving somewhere deep in the black.

"Can I have a cigarette?"

"What? Oh, yeah."

He handed her his pack. She stared at it before shaking one free. She rolled the single smoke between her fingers. "I like the little penguin above the filter."

Lonnie exchanged cigarettes for Zippo. "Were you in the army?" she asked, staring at the lighter.

"Yeah."

"Fight in the war?"

"Korea? Yeah."

"Nobody talks much about Korea. You kill anybody?"

He hated that question and couldn't understand why everyone asked it. "It was a war," he said.

"I know," she said. "But sometimes people say they were in the war, but they weren't *in* the war. And the people who were? Did they think about actually killing someone?"

Lonnie nodded. He hadn't. The mechanics of war never occurred to him when he signed his papers. All the bodies entombed in history books, those were just numbers. None were people.

"What was it like?"

"Killing?" He hated that question more. "You shouldn't be asking about things like that."

"Why?" She stuck the cigarette in her mouth and made googly eyes. "Cause I'm a girl?"

Because I don't want you to be like everyone else, he thought. "No. It's just…"

"Would you have killed those men?" She lit her cigarette. "The bikers?" She dragged hard.

"I—"

"God, what *are* these?" She stuck her tongue out, made a yuck face.

"Kools with a k," he said.

"Taste funny."

"They're mentholated. Good for your throat and your T-zone or something."

Daisy watched the smoke curl from the end of her cigarette. She took another smaller drag to be sure, then said, grimacing, "I don't like them."

"Nat King Cole smokes 'em."

"Well, my whore mother smokes Fatimas and those are awful too." She took the cigarette from her mouth and tossed it into the tide. The water carried it half a foot from shore, looped it back a few inches from her feet, and then slapped it against her shoe.

Daisy ground it into the sand. "You ever feel like everything beautiful dies?"

Lonnie sucked air like the salt could boil out his soul. *Yeah,* he thought, remembering the bodies stacked like wood, *I do,* and he was angry again. Angry at everything. Angry that there was no one to blame or hold accountable but a faceless universe and that only made everything worse.

Daisy faced him. Her boy's shirt had slipped down her back, the collar hung by her shoulder blades like malformed wings. "Maybe that's why it's all so fucking pretty sometimes?"

Lonnie blinked.

Daisy sat down beside him on the sand with her knees against her chest. "You hear about that guy in Nebraska?"

"What guy?"

"The killer. The one who's going to be executed."

"Starkweather?"

"Yeah, what do you think about him and the girl?" She crab walked to drier sand.

"What do you mean?"

"They're killers, right? No one says different. But what about them, together?"

"Don't know what you mean."

"Papers say all kinds of stuff about whose idea it was. Hers. His. Both."

"No one knows but her and Starkweather." *And the dead*, Lonnie thought. *They always know.*

"Yeah, but what do *you* think?"

"Don't know, Daisy."

"You've gotta have a thought, right?"

He had too many. "I can see why you're still waiting for a husband," he said and regretted it.

"Not the first time I've heard that."

He sighed. "All right," he said, "I think it was him. Don't think she knew what was going to happen. It was kicks before it was killing. Went too far. Got outta hand. She didn't know what to do. Lotsa things like that. You end up somewhere you didn't expect but you're too afraid to do anything, to go back or forward." He tossed his butt in the ocean and lit another, finishing over the flame and through bursts of smoke, "Mostly, I think they killed people and it doesn't matter who said or who did what."

Daisy nodded. "Want to know what I think?"

He didn't say anything, but he did.

"I think they were two lonely and broken people who found each other and were happy for a moment and crushed whatever threatened it."

"Does it matter? They're both guilty."

"Maybe not," she said. "I like my story better."

Lonnie liked her story better too. He wanted it to be true, but, "It's not," he told her.

"You don't know."

"I do."

"You don't. You weren't there. You said it earlier—no one knows but her and Starkweather."

"You weren't there either."

"I know." She rested her chin on her knees and stared down her legs at her damp sneakers. "Your thing's probably the truth. Hell, it is the truth.

Most things are a lot simpler than we make them. But I don't like your answer. I like mine better. A lot better." She tugged on his jeans. "Maybe that's
all we can do, Lonnie Bonner from Kentucky? Find something good out of
all the bad. Find someone. Someone as broken as we are."

"Two broken things?"

"Yeah. Maybe they make a whole thing." She brushed her hair from
her face, tugged it around her ears and held it under her chin. "If only for
a minute. And sometimes a minute is enough. We know all our answers
already, Lonnie Bonner. We just need to accept them."

He turned from her and flicked his cigarette in a high arch. As it hit
the waves and sank, she said, "My father told me that when he divorced
my mother. It's the only thing that keeps me from hating him completely."

They watched the waves and listened to the wind, like either could tell
them of something other than their own insignificance.

Lonnie wanted to hold her hand. He didn't know how long it had
been since he wanted that. To hold a girl's hand. That desire broke what
remained of his heart.

When the thought became too much for him, another sound rumbled
over the thunderous pounding of the surf. Lonnie looked out over the
ocean, thinking it came from somewhere out there, but fearing that it had
in fact come from somewhere inside.

He thought then that Daisy was saying something, but when he turned
he saw she wasn't. She was looking back toward the cliff. He followed her
eyes and saw five motorcycles racing down the winding road to the beach.

"You ever surfed?"

"No."

"Me neither. I wish I knew how to surf like Gidget. I'd get away," Daisy
said.

The motorcycles hit the shore, spraying sand and racing toward his
Ford. When they were even with the coupe, the Triumph pulled away, roar-
ing down the beach and skidding to a halt between them and the car. The
rider climbed off his bike, lit a cigarette and waited while his gang circled
the coupe, whooping and hollering before falling in line behind him.

Lonnie reached down and pulled Daisy to her feet. She met his eyes as
she stood. He turned away from her sad resignation and stared at her hand
in his. Her fingers were splayed and bent against his palm. He squeezed and
held them tight for a moment, until they straightened. "Stay behind me,
Daisy," he said, releasing her hand and walking toward the pack.

Lonnie marked positions and named targets as he approached: Sideburns, Big Ears, Glasses, and Shorty. But it was the Triumph's rider he eyeballed. The leader wore dirty jeans, engineer boots, and a battered leather jacket. His hair was cut in a flat-top boogie, long and greased smooth on the sides, short and spiky on top.

Sideburns spoke first. "This is our beach, daddy-o."

Glasses grinned. "Yeah, we tried to tell you earlier."

"Just let us go." Lonnie looked over his shoulder at Daisy and nodded at the coupe. "We were leaving."

"Yeah, split, man. Split." Big Ears laughed.

Flat-Top pointed at Daisy. "Split, but leave the girl."

Glasses reached for her. Daisy jerked her hand away before he could touch it. "We missed you earlier." He grinned, the thick glasses distorting his eyes like a comic book novelty. "She's swell."

Lonnie moved between them. Put a hand on leather. "Leave her alone."

Flat-top tongued his cigarette to the right side of his mouth and blew smoke out the left. "You her boyfriend?"

The men fanned out in a wide semi-circle. Lonnie retreated, keeping Daisy behind him, directing her with his arm. There weren't enough to surround them, but they'd make reaching the car trouble.

"Her brother?"

"They don't look alike," Shorty said, moving farther off to Lonnie's right. "This sonofabitch is backwoods ugly."

"No," Lonnie said.

Flat-top gestured wildly. "Then what the fuck is it to you?"

Lonnie looked at the older man. He didn't like the dark familiarity he saw in his eyes, but he tried to speak to it. "Come on. One vet to another."

Flat-top looked at his gang. He scissored the smoke from his lips with his right hand. He nodded, then looked at Daisy as he raised it for another long drag. "You're a vet?" He stepped forward and unzipped his leather. "Of what?"

"Korea," Lonnie said.

The gang scoffed.

Flat-Top spit out his cig and handed his jacket to Glasses, who draped it across his handlebars. The white t-shirt underneath was dusty and dirty, stained with blood and whiskey and road grit. Boardwalk tattoos covered each wide forearm. "Omaha Beach."

"15th Infantry," Lonnie said. "We covered the X Corps withdrawal at

Chosin and defended Outpost Harry." *Fuck you and your beach*, he thought. *You would have shit your pants at Chosin and cried at the Teeth.*

Shorty chuckled. "Yeah, you failed, man. Ko-rea is what? Half-communist now?"

"That's not failure. It's a draw," Daisy said.

Sideburns darted, caught her arm, and wrenched her close. "Shut the fuck up, Mary Reed, or I'll tell Donna."

Lonnie's eyes moved quickly through the crowd. "She's not with you. Let her go."

Flat-Top nodded. Sideburns released her wrist and rolled his shoulders. "Fuck you, man," he said.

Lonnie saw how this was going to go. He knew Flat-top read it too. The gang leader looked at him and said, "What do you got?"

Lonnie shrugged. He glanced at Daisy, then back at the biker. "Not a lot."

Flat-Top chuckled. "You and me. For her. No one else. You. Me. For her."

Lonnie wished he could signal Daisy to run. Knowing it would be square only as long as the fight went in the gang's favor, he didn't like his odds. *Fuck it*—"Brando sucks dick."

Flat-top hit him in the corner of the mouth. Lonnie felt his lip bust, and he staggered back in the sand, pivoting and trying not to fall. Sideburns saved him the effort and clocked him from the other side. Lonnie's ass brushed sand, but he quickly back-peddled up to his feet and shrugged it off. He saw someone—maybe Daisy—running across the beach. He tried to spit, found his balance, and looped a wild swing at Flat-Top. The gang leader ducked, came up quick and popped him another one in the mouth. As Lonnie reeled, he punched blindly and landed a solid almost-hook on his jaw.

Flat-top's head snapped sharp right. Lonnie stumbled close and swung to the gut hoping for a liver shot. The gang leader saw it coming. He tensed and turned, feinting an uppercut to hide a dirty elbow. Lonnie ate it willingly as he torqued his waist and extended his fist, hammering a solid blow into Flat-top's belly. The force sent ripples through the gang leader's abdominals.

Flat-Top staggered back. Lonnie pressed forward. He swung again toward the body only to change directions and hook the jaw. The blow landed solid. The shock dropped Flat-Top's hands. Lonnie saw his chance.

He head-butted him, then rammed three more body blows home.

When their leader drooled blood and fell, the gang wolf-packed him.

Someone landed a glancing blow to Lonnie's temple. He took it, blinked, and ducked, firing a stiff jab. He felt it hit, but not as hard as the counter punch that cracked his nose.

Tears filled his eyes. He swung at anything, trying to keep distance and not get mobbed.

Hands shoved him, a stiff finger jabbed his eye.

Lonnie punched schoolyard style, formless and crazy.

Shorty grabbed his shirt and tried to pull him down. Lonnie clawed at hands while kicks pummeled his legs. He tried to push back, but a brass-knuckled fist slammed into his exposed rib and he cried out, went to a knee and wrenched. His shirt ripped and he punched, hoping for dick but right-crossing only bony thigh.

A boot slammed into his spine and he dropped forward, nearly falling on his face before a looping swing clacked his teeth together.

Sideburns pushed them back.

Lonnie swayed on his knees. He looked at the dirty faces surrounding him. He breathed once, willed himself to stand. "Fuck all ya all," he slurred, raising his hands weakly to guard.

Sideburns grinned. The mutton-chopped biker swung his arms wide to gesture for more room. When the space around him cleared, he slid a switchblade from his back pocket and raised it eye height with a flourish. "First, we stick you." A slow button push popped the blade free. "Then we stick her."

For a second, Lonnie didn't know where he was or what was going on. Sideburns brandished the knife and smiled. Lonnie blinked, rolled his shoulders and said, "Gonna shove that in your ass, you mealy-mouthed motherfucker."

Sideburns curled his lips and showed his teeth. "Don't know which sticking I'm gonna like more," he said and slashed.

Lonnie hopped back but stumbled over his own feet. The point of the blade split the skin along his thumb. He bit his lip to keep silent and hooked at a big chop.

His punch hit only leather-clad shoulder.

Sideburns countered with his knife and nicked Lonnie's exposed side.

Winded and dazed, Lonnie kicked, hit nothing, and followed with something like a punch.

Sideburns slashed the air madly, laughing and giggling with his wide mouth covered in spittle.

The two circled and circled, until Lonnie bled from hundreds of little cuts up and down his arms.

Finally, he moved quickly away, shaking his arms out to lessen the sting and hoping to break their unconscious rhythm. When he retreated, Shorty punched him in his back, a knuckle left of spine. The blow stopped him.

The diminutive gang member snaked his hands around Lonnie's arms and pined them, yelling, "Bleed him! Bleed the motherfucker!"

Sideburns grinned. He thrust the blade, and the shotgun boomed above the surf.

The gang looked in the direction of the shot. Daisy stood in front of the coupe, flanked by the burning headlights. "Let him go!"

"Put it down!" Flat-Top yelled, winced.

Daisy shook her head. She raised the gun.

The gang waited on Flat-top's order.

"Last time." He stepped, the gang tensed. "Won't say it again. Put it down."

Daisy pumped the shell free and braced the stock against her shoulder. "No."

"You little—" He started to run and Daisy fired. Her aim was wide left, but with the barrel chopped she hit. The pellets tore across the outer meat of Flat-Top's thigh and dropped him howling to the sand.

Daisy pumped the shell loose, chambering her next load. She took a step of her own, sweeping the shotgun over the others, then fired once more in the air. "Let him the fuck go!"

Shorty released his hold. Lonnie dropped to his knees, then fell backward onto his back.

Sideburns raised his wet blade and pointed. "Fuck you, you blue-jeaned bitch."

Daisy cleared the spent shell and sighted, locking the shotgun on Sideburns. He tried to stand tall even as his friends backed away, but nothing could hide the bend growing in his knees, the shake spreading up his legs.

"You're a dead man," she said and slowly squeezed.

Sideburns dropped.

Daisy swung the gun toward his bike and fired. The shotgun pellets riddled the tank, popped the front tire, and punched the bike over.

Sideburns howled and beat the sand with his fists.

Daisy chambered. "Get the fuck out of here!"

The gang stared.

Flat-Top moaned.

Daisy yelled again.

And now they moved, slow to their feet and creeping out of caution toward their downed leader, plodding with deliberate malice.

"Get out of here!" She fired at the sky. "Get the fuck out of here!" Cleared the chamber. "I swear to God, I'll kill you. I see any one of you again, and I'll blow you to hell."

Lonnie turned his face toward the shore as the bikes roared to life. The ocean remained unchanged. Waves rose and fell. Rose and fell. Rose and fell.

He watched until the whine of the engines quieted and his head lulled back cliffside. He saw Daisy walking toward him with her head down. She laid the shotgun on the sand, then stepped away like she had gotten caught playing with something she wasn't supposed to. "My father used to take me skeet shooting," she said.

Lonnie turned his face to the sky. It was cold and empty. "How'd you know?"

Daisy stepped forward, blocking his view of the thoughtless heavens. "I saw it when I leaned in your window," she said, fretting the jagged skin along her thumbnail. "And you left a box of shells in the front floorboard."

He breathed heavy, releasing a long sigh. Daisy stuck her hand out. "You're bleeding," she said.

Lonnie took her hand. She grunted, helped him to his feet, and then, before he knew why she was leaning in close, she kissed him on the mouth sweetly. "We should get a dog," she said, pulling her lips far enough away to speak. "He could ride with us. He could sit in the back. I'd name him Bandit, and he'd wear a bandana around his neck. One I bought at a roadside place from a nice old lady who thought we were married. You'd think it was too expensive—the bandana, not the dog. He'd like me better, of course. He'd protect me when you were gone."

She pressed her lips into his again. Lonnie loved her right then. Part of him knew it was silly. Most of him didn't care. It was worth it to be whole—even for only a minute.

SCARRED ANGEL
HEATH LOWRANCE

See: Fast-living hot rod girls in action!
Witness: Violent teen crime spree!
Experience: Unbridled teenage passion out of control!

She presses her high-heeled shoe into the gas pedal. The Corvette leaps forward and the cops fall far behind. She laughs maniacally, the wind whips her jet-black hair away from her face, and the scar that runs from her temple to her jaw glows white in the dashboard lights.

She tears her eyes away from the road long enough to glance at me. I see the wild craziness in them and my heart lurches. She says, "You and me, baby. Right? If we have to die tonight, we die together!"

After it was all over, the newspapers called her Frankie Scar, which maybe boosted circulation but was goddamn mean-natured if you ask me. There was a lot more to Frankie than that scar, and it sort of made me mad that they'd reduce her to something so meaningless, so cosmetic, as the scar on her face.

I knew her, see. I mean, really knew her. You probably saw that magazine story called "The Boy Who Loved Frankie Scar." Yeah, that was me. Not surprising that the story would be full of lies, though. I mean, yeah, I did love her. I loved her with a burn in my heart, the kind of love that squares would never understand.

But almost everything else they got totally wrong.

She was leaning up against the counter at Jimmy Bo's, smoking a cigarette and glaring at everyone. I was with Kurt and Sonny, the three of us in a booth nursing milkshakes like a bunch of kids. We all noticed her at the same time.

Sonny said, "Wowsie! Check out the filly!"

Me and Kurt were already checking out the filly. So was everyone else.

She was a tight little package of dynamite in a dark blue sweater and a black skirt. The sweater hugged curves that would put you up on two wheels. She had long black hair that hung down over her right eye like Lizabeth Scott. She smoked her cigarette like she hated it, with naked disdain all over her china white face.

"Go on, Scotty," Sonny said to me. "You're always complaining about not having a steady. Here's your chance."

I flushed. "No dice. That doll is out of my league."

"Nonsense, my good man," Kurt said in that goofy British accent he'd been doing ever since he saw *The Bridge On The River Kwai* earlier that year. "No young lady is beyond your multitude of personal chahms, good suh."

"Knock it off, Alec Guinness," I said, and they laughed.

In his normal voice, Kurt said, "But really, Scotty, you should swing for it. What do you have to lose?"

"My dignity."

"You have dignity? When did that happen?"

They ribbed me for a few minutes while the doll finished her cigarette, tossed it on the floor and rubbed it out with the toe of one high-heeled shoe. I was looking at her gams. They were long and smooth and shaped about perfect. She wasn't wearing stockings.

She glanced over at me and our eyes met. Something flickered in my gut. The disdain on her face vanished for a split-second.

Next thing I knew, I was on my feet and walking toward her.

•••

It was all I could do to maintain my James Dean with her, but I pulled it off. I asked if I could buy her a milkshake, and she sighed and said sure like she wasn't too thrilled with the prospect. She ordered a chocolate malted, then took one sip from the straw and left it melting on the counter top.

It's hard to be cool and find out about a girl at the same time. A real cool cat wouldn't ask questions; he wouldn't care. But I'm not really that cool.

She, on the other hand, was ice.

When I asked her name, she said, "Frankie."

"As in Francis?"

"As in Frankie."

She didn't ask my name. She put another cigarette between her pouty lips, looked at me, and I fumbled for the lighter in my jeans pocket. I didn't really smoke much, but always kept a pack and a Zippo with me for appearance's sake. I lit her up and she took a deep drag, let out smoke and said, "Let's blow this joint. Milkshakes are for squares. I know where we can get a bottle."

I almost said a bottle of what before catching myself.

...

We started to head toward the Ford my pop let me use for the night. She put a hand on my arm. "You're joking, right?" she said. "We'll take my wheels." Her wheels were a souped-up '57 Corvette convertible, canary yellow. I couldn't help whistling. That model only came out the year before and I only ever saw one in *Popular Mechanics*.

"Now that's a ride."

"Damn straight, youngster," she grinned, and it was as animated as I'd seen her so far.

She got behind the wheel and I jumped in the passenger seat. Next thing I know we're squealing out of Jimmy-Bo's parking lot onto the street.

She shifted gears and the V-8 roared. We were a streak of yellow and black. We veered around slow traffic, tagged the stop light, and she made a hard turn right. Rubber screamed. She shifted gears again and in a heartbeat we were up to 90 miles an hour on the main strip.

My heart was in my throat. I glanced over at her and she had this look on her face, like the look I'd seen on the faces of people in church when they got the Holy Spirit in them.

And then I saw the scar.

Her shining black hair had hidden it before, but now the wind had whipped it all back behind her head. The scar ran jagged from her temple all the way down to her jaw. My breath caught in my throat. But it wasn't what you think. I wasn't repulsed.

She risked a quick look at me and I knew I was grinning like a sick fool, full of terror and excitement and lust. She winked at me and the lust took a giant leap forward into love or something like it.

She had the Corvette humming, changing lanes smooth as a baby's belly, other cars standing still in our wake. They were honking at us as we sped past, but they were almost like stationary objects and the sounds they made were gone almost before I could hear them.

A prowler lurked at the corner of Main and Front. We roared by him and he hit his cop siren and took off after us.

She pushed for more speed and tickled the 105 MPH mark. The cop didn't stand a chance. In less than three seconds he was way behind us. Frankie laughed like a lunatic. She touched the brakes lightly right before 4th Street and down-shifted. We squealed into the turn, backend almost fish-tailing before she got it under control. Her high heel pumped the clutch, her small white hand shifted up and we were tearing away.

Goddamn, that girl could drive!

After a few miles, 4th turned into Forest Road, and we were well past the outskirts of town. I used to think it was a long haul out of the city and into the rural area surrounding it. Not anymore. It took less than five minutes with Frankie at the wheel. The road opened up in front of us and there weren't many cars now. The sun was going down, burning huge and orange. It felt like the end of the world. It was a good feeling.

Just outside the county line, there was a juke joint along the side of the road. I'd seen it before but never paid much attention to it. It was a Negro place, not suitable for whites. But Frankie slowed down and turned into the gravel parking lot. Dust billowed under the wheels and she parked behind an old, beat-up Coupe De Ville.

"Well?" she said. "Coming?"

It was dark inside. There was a short bar made of plywood and a few sawhorse tables. The jukebox played Jackie Brenston's "Rocket 88". Everything smelled like cigarette smoke and burnt corn. I also caught a quick whiff of reefer in the air. I knew the smell because, last year, me and Sonny and Kurt actually tried some. They had gotten goofy on it, but it just sort of gave me a headache.

The Negroes barely looked at us when we came in. I didn't know if I was expecting a race riot or something, but I was relieved that they didn't seem to care about these two white kids in their midst.

Frankie sashayed over to the bar, said to the bartender, "How's tricks, Elmore?"

He said, "Fine and dandy, Miss Frankie. The usual?"

She nodded and he slid a bottle across the bar. She grabbed it, looked at me, and said, "I'm a little light, baby. You get this?"

I came out of my stupor enough to say, "Huh? Oh, yeah. No sweat." I pulled a couple bills out of my pocket and put them on the bar without really looking at them. I was afraid to hand them directly to the bartender for some reason.

He grinned, swooped up the bills. "I never had nobody pay ten bucks for a bottle before," he said. "But if that's what it's worth to you, I ain't complaining."

I felt like a sap, but Frankie only laughed. She cracked open the bottle, took a swig right out of it, and handed it to me. I followed her example. I'd half-expected some rotgut but it was actually good whiskey, as good as the stuff my pop kept in his cabinet. It burned and glowed in my chest and stomach, and I instantly felt better about everything in the world.

I handed her the bottle. She said, "'atta boy," and put her arm around my waist.

The song on the jukebox shifted to the opening piano chords of a Fats Domino number, "Whole Lotta Loving", and Frankie's eyes got wide. "Dance!" she said. "Come on!" She grabbed my arm and pulled me out into the middle of the place where a bunch of other people were already dancing.

I'm a pretty self-conscious dancer usually, but her enthusiasm was contagious, and after less than a minute I wasn't even thinking about how stupid I looked anymore. I just danced with Frankie and let myself go while Fats crooned, "Gotta whole lotta lovin'... for you, true, true lovin'... for you, I gotta whole lotta lovin' for you..."

The way Frankie danced, it was like she was calling up the spirits of the dead. It made me think about a film I saw once of some primitive jungle tribe, dancing around a fire. Primal and intense. Her eyes were closed, and her rounded hips swayed and bucked, slower than the music, but perfectly in synch. The bottle was forgotten in her hand. She was hypnotized, and so was I, watching her.

No one else paid attention. They'd given her a space, a respectful distance. No one looked at us, and I felt so connected to her at that moment that the juke-joint faded away and for the short duration of the song nothing else existed except me and Frankie, dancing.

The song was short, too short. I felt like it could've gone on another four hours and I would've been fine, lost in a moment that stretched and stretched all the way to infinity.

The juke transitioned to a Little Anthony and the Imperials tune, "Tears on My Pillow." Frankie barely opened her eyes. She moved into me, her arms snaking up over my shoulders, and her head against my chest. Our bodies pressed together and we barely moved as the slow number played out.

When the song was over, she pushed away from me, took a long swig from the bottle. She looked at me funny, a strange light in her dark eyes.

Then she said, "Come on, let's sit down. No more of this sappy stuff."

•••

We finished the bottle there at the juke joint, dancing sometimes when Frankie got the itch, but mostly we just sat and drank. When the bottle was done, Frankie said, "Why don't you pop for another bottle, baby? And then we'll get out of here."

I was half-drunk from the five or six swigs of whiskey I've had. Frankie killed most of the bottle, but she seemed right as rain. I stumbled up to the bar, got another bottle, and we were off.

It was full-on dark outside. I looked at my watch for the first time all night.

Two in the morning.

"Holy cow," I said, before I could stop myself. Frankie arched an eyebrow at me, and I didn't tell her about how my folks were going to read me the riot act when I got home. That would've been painfully square.

I had no idea then that I wouldn't be going home again, ever.

Instead, I grinned at her and said, "What now, doll?"

"Sleep. I'm dead on my feet."

"Oh. Okay. You think you can, you know, drop me back in town? At Jimmy-Bo's?"

"Now why would I do that, baby?"

We got in the car and she peeled out, heading away from town. I decided to let it go. Who knew what was going to happen next with this doll? It would probably be worth the hell I was sure to catch from the parents.

•••

"Listen," she said, lying down on the bed. "I know how this looks and I know you're probably getting all sorts of ideas. But I don't want to be touched. So no funny business, okay?"

I was lying next to her. Looking up at the ceiling, I said, "That's okay. No problem. I have amazing self-control."

But I'd be a liar if I said I wasn't disappointed. From the moment she'd suggested stopping at this cheap little motel, I'd had a raging woody, had thought, *Holy cow, I'm actually going to get some action!*...but it was not to be, I guess.

I was seventeen and had only ever been with one girl before, about six months earlier. Suzy Peroni was a sixteen year old with a bad reputation, and she'd moved to another state only a week later. It was a point of embarrassment for me since both Sonny and Kurt had been with three or four girls each…to hear them tell it, anyway.

Girls, man…they just made me feel awkward and stupid.

But I was starting to feel comfortable with Frankie. The fact that this stunningly beautiful girl wanted to spend time with me—even if we were only just lying there and not touching each other—made me feel sort of like a big shot.

Maybe it was her scar. Maybe that was why she was hanging around with me instead of some tough, leather jacket-wearing bad boy. Maybe no one else could see past it to the magnificent creature she was.

I wanted to ask her about the scar right then, but I heard her snoring very softly, and when I looked at her, her eyes were closed and all the hardness had left her face. She was an angel.

She was my scar-faced and raven-haired bad, bad angel.

...

I asked her the next morning. It was after ten and I knew my folks were probably having conniptions about now, but you know what? I didn't care anymore. All the grief in the world was worth it.

Frankie woke up slow and groggy. She stretched luxuriously on the bed and her skirt hiked up. I could see the frilly panties she wore underneath and her full white thighs. I wanted so bad to touch her. But I didn't. Instead, I sat on the edge of the bed and said, "Can I ask you something?"

"The scar, right?" she mumbled.

"If you don't want to… I mean, it's none of my business, I guess. I just—"

She touched the scar, ran a finger over it. "It's a going-away present," she said. "From my Daddy."

"Oh."

"First, he did things to me that a Daddy shouldn't do to his daughter. And then, when I fought back, he grabbed his straight razor and sliced my face."

"Jesus Christ."

She sat up, yawned, and put her head against my chest. "It's ugly, isn't it?"

"No," I said, and I meant it. "It's you. It's part of you, of what you've experienced. I love it."

She cocked an eyebrow at me. "You love it? That's just weird."

"I don't care if it's weird. I love it. I love everything about you."

A little tenderness came into her eyes and she touched my face very gently. For a second I thought she was going to kiss me. But she didn't. In-stead, she said, "Weirdo," then got out of bed and headed for the bathroom to take a shower.

...

We stopped at a roadside diner, and I sprung for coffee and waffles. Frankie ate like a truck driver, elbows on the table, not looking at me and not talking. When she was done, she lit a smoke and said, "So, baby… you're getting a little light in the wallet by now, aren't you?"

I shrugged, not wanting to admit it. I wondered if me being stony meant she was done with me. But she only said, "Hmm. We'll have to do something about that."

When we left the diner, we drove around the countryside for a couple of hours, just letting the sun shine down on us and the wind blast our faces. We didn't talk much. Two or three times, though, she reached over and put her hand on mine, removing it only when she had to shift gears.

By one o'clock, we were in the next county. We pulled in front of a run-down liquor store. She parked the Corvette and said, "Do me a favor, baby, and reach into the glove box for me?"

I popped it open.

There was a gun in there, an ugly looking snub-nosed revolver.

"Hand me that, would you?" she said. "Unless you want to do the honors?"

"What?"

"Gonna need the gun to rob this guy, baby."

"Rob this guy? Wait a minute, what are you talking about?"

"You're out of spending cash, and so am I. But the problem, see, is that I'm not quite done having a ball yet. And to have a ball, one requires bread."

"You're gonna rob the liquor store? Holy cow, Frankie."

She eyeballed me, said, "Don't be a wet rag, baby. Hand me the gun."

I took it out of the glove compartment and handed it to her.

Grinning, she opened her door and started to get out. But then she stopped very suddenly, leaned over and kissed me on the cheek. "Come on, baby," she said. "This'll be radioactive."

...

The guy running the place was leafing through a girlie magazine and barely looked at us when we came in. He was an old geezer with a buzz cut and a big fat mustache like one of those villains in an old cheese-ball

Western. Frankie walked right by him, swinging her hips to beat the band, the gun tucked into her skirt.

She grabbed a bottle of good whiskey off the shelf, me right behind her sweating bullets. At the counter, the geezer looked up from his magazine, seemed to notice for the first time that he was face-to-face with a living doll. He said, "Oh. Will, uh, will that be all, little missy?"

She tossed her head back, letting her curtain of gorgeous black hair sweep away so he could see the scar on her face. He turned white, and Frankie said, "No, not quite, Clyde." She pulled out the revolver. "I'll also be liberating you of all your bread."

"What... what do you mean by this?"

"Your bread, Dad. Your cash. Your money." He only stared at her, and she barked, "Money! Now, you fucking asshole!"

That one shocked me and the clerk both. I'd heard the "f"-word before, of course—my Pop came back from the Pacific very well-versed in its use—but I'd never, ever heard a female say it before. It was like getting punched in the face.

She leveled the gun at his face and he finally started moving, opening up the cash register and scooping out all the bills. He put them on the counter, and Frankie said, "Baby, grab this dough."

I did what she said, grabbing it up and shoving it all in my pockets. I was numb.

"That's all of it," the geezer said, his eyes locked on Frankie's face.

Frankie said, "What are you looking at, Clyde?"

"Nothin', miss, I just—"

"You looking at my scar, you old bastard? What, you like it? You one of those degenerate old bastards who get all hot over scars?"

"No, missy, I was only... that is—"

"Well, you can't touch me," Frankie said, her face twisted with rage. "You can't touch me and neither can my father and neither can anyone, you understand? No one can touch me unless I say so."

"I don't wanna touch you, missy."

"No one controls me, you understand, Clyde? No one. I'm not one of your little hussy housewives or preening, stupid teeny-boppers, you got me? I'm in control of me, no one else!"

Tears of anger were coursing down her face. I wasn't looking at the geezer anymore, but at her, at my Frankie. My heart pounded hard in my chest and I knew, I just knew what was going to happen, but I made no move to stop it.

Hell, I wanted her to do it by then. I wanted her to show them all.

And she did. She pulled the trigger and shot the old geezer right in the head.

•••

We burned rubber out of there, and I pulled all the money out of my pockets as she drove. It scattered all over the floorboards. I started gathering it all up.

It was about a hundred and eighty bucks. That old bastard had died for less than two hundred clams.

But no. That wasn't all he died for. I glanced over at Frankie, her make-up streaked with tears and mascara running down her cheeks, and I knew that the geezer had died for all the sins committed against my scarred angel. He died as penance for a hand laid on her against her will.

She drove the Corvette hard for thirty miles, deep into the farmland and scattered forests of the county. At a graveled side road, she yanked the wheel and tore away from the main road, gravel and dust spewing up behind us. She spotted a shady area just big enough to pull the car into and slammed on the brakes inches from a big oak tree.

She looked at me, breathing heavy.

And then she slid across the seat, grabbed my face in both hands and pulled me to her. We kissed hard enough to hurt my teeth and her tongue darted against mine. Next thing I knew my hands were under her sweater, cupping her breasts, and she fell back into the seat, pulling me down with her. She hiked up her skirt, and I pulled her panties down as she fumbled at my belt buckle.

We made love there, with the stolen money on the floorboard and the branches of the oak tree dropping leaves down on my naked back and the smell of gunpowder still clinging to her.

•••

One hundred and eighty wasn't enough.

"We need more," Frankie said. "At least five hundred. If we're gonna get out of this state in style, that is."

"What do you suggest?"

She grinned at me and wet her lips, then kissed me on the nose. "There's no shortage of liquor stores, baby. And I'll tell you what—next time, you get to hold the gun."

We robbed another store that evening, without fatalities this time, because I held the gun. Frankie did all the talking, but I was the one with the weapon. After we got away, we pulled over and made love again, just as desperately, just as violently.

The next morning, we hit another one.

We found an empty field, tall with wheat-grass, and afterwards I said to her, "Frankie. I love you."

"I know, baby. I love you, too. With all my heart."

Loaded with cash, we headed toward the state line and listened to the news on the radio. The cops were after us by now. They didn't have an I.D. on Frankie—she was the "raven-haired harlot, kept from being beautiful by a hideous scar". But me—they had me pegged. Scotty Brown, seventeen years old, high school senior and track star. Never in trouble in his entire life. A good kid. They talked to my parents, right there on the radio. My Mom sounded tearful and scared. She begged me to give it up and come home and surely whatever the problem was it could be resolved.

Frankie looked at me and said, "What do you say, baby? You wanna go back home and hug your poor old mama?"

I flipped off the radio. "No," I said. "Fuck all of them."

Frankie laughed and laughed and laughed.

...

There was a roadblock at the state line. That was where they got us.

We barreled through it, sending cops scattering for safety in all directions, and tore up the highway with the cruisers right on our tail. They couldn't catch us that way, we knew. But we also knew they would be in front of us too. And they were.

County cops and state troopers were all over the road, zipping in from the sides, lights flashing and sirens deafening. Not looking away from the road, Frankie said, "The gun, baby. Use the gun."

I did, leaning out the window and shooting in the direction of the cops behind us. I didn't hit anyone, didn't try to. It was enough to feel the gun bucking in my hand, the roar as it barked out bullets. It was enough to know the cops thought I was trying to kill them.

They started shooting back. The windshield of the Corvette spider-webbed as a bullet smashed into it. Another shot whined off the door inches from my arm.

I turned to Frankie. "I think it's over, doll."

She nodded and some of the mad glee went out of her. She looked sad. "I know," she said.

But then she pressed the gas and the wind tore at our faces and she laughed again. We were both so alive at that moment, it was overwhelming. She said, "You and me, baby. Right? If we have to die tonight, we die together!"

A bullet caught her in the back of the head.

She didn't make a sound, just slumped against the wheel and the Corvette careened out of control at 100 miles an hour. It leapt off the highway and into the ditch, crashed into a tree, and I was flying through the air with glass shards in my face and chest and I couldn't feel anything.

I slammed into the tree head-first and the world went black.

...

I attend my trial in a wheelchair. My lawyer tries to use the fact that I'll never walk again to convince the jury that I've paid for my crimes. He points out the hideous scars on my face and my obviously broken spirit. The jury ain't having any of it.

I get twenty years. Lawyer says he thinks I'll be out in seven, with good behavior. I don't care.

I like to look in the mirror and study my scars now. Every one of them reminds me of Frankie, and so I love them.

At night in my cell, I sleep and I dream about her, about her long black hair and her lovely scar. I miss her so much I can hardly stand it.

When I get out of here, I'm going to pay a little visit to her dad and see what he has to say about things.

HEADLESS HOGGY STYLE
DAVID JAMES KEATON

"I'm a hard hallucinator with an axe to grind,
shooting from the hip like a porcupine…"
- "Mutha Fukka On A Motorcycle"—Machine Gun Fellatio

Jake pulled his gloves slow and tight like a doctor in a horror flick and kick-started his bike. He revved the engine loud, louder, louder, the rumble growing deep in his chest, then moving up to thrum the tuning fork of his spine to finally nest in his brain. He looked both ways down the intersection, then leaned back and gave Cherry a last kiss on the red apple of her cheek. He cranked the throttle and raced through the next two lights before they changed, angling his wheel for the rotten tomato stand and the yawning mouth of the abandoned corn maze behind it.

But they never got there. Jake saw the blur of something he took for a wooden baseball bat jamming into his spokes and exploding into toothpicks as he lost the bull rope of his handlebars between his legs and rode the fender onto the street. The gong of his brain bucket painted his world black a second or two, eardrums rattling like an old man's newspaper. Then he sat up on the road, counted his heads, and started flicking stones embedded deep as ticks from his face. When he finally focused, he looked around for Cherry's splashdown, and that's when the hairy fist found the hole under his nose and sent him flying back into his shredded saddle. Rolling to his feet, Jake flailed for a weapon, hoping to find a shard of the bat, maybe with the "slugger" stamp still visible, but there was nothing but confetti and paper in his spokes, ticking like playing cards as the wheel spun. Later, he realized he'd been taken down by grass-stained stakes and a rolled poster urging people to vote for the local noise ordinance. Exactly the kind of shit that turned farmers murderous. But it wasn't a farmer that clipped him this time, he was sure of it. Kicking away the poster strips, he stood up to find the owner of the fist long gone and tried to pinpoint the buzz of a dozen dirt bikes in the distance. Suddenly remembering the love of his life may have ended her run as a comet trail along the Morse code of white lines, his pulse spiked.

It took a good ten minutes more before he was sure his bike was drivable and his heart finally slowed back down.

...

Fingers bloody from shucking strings off guitars, they're sitting on the hood of Jake's '57 Eldorado, holding hands and enjoying the show. Cherry always liked watching red police lights flash in the distance. He calls these lights "cherries," too, but everything's cherry to him these days. They're on a hill, overlooking a lopsided crop circle. The cops have found the first body, still clutching 100cc's of Baja motocross nonsense. But she's playing her own game, too. Not just refusing to answer the question anymore, she's stopped speaking altogether. But it's hard for him not to ask the question, and it squirts out of him again before he realizes.

"What are you thinking?"

He can't help it, watching her watching cops from the hill with her cold, button eyes. He wishes they could hear them crunching the dead, brown stalks, figuring it all out, maybe see flashlight beams crisscross their faces as they kiss. He wonders if she's thinking of the 4th of July, the red and blue fireworks and their second kiss, their first real kiss. He thinks about how she watched the shirtless men lighting the rockets instead of watching the explosions and how he hoped she was waiting for someone to get hurt.

Jake squeezes her hand the wrong way, watching those doll's eyes for a reaction. Nothing. He knows it's his fault. Sure, he promised never to ask that question again, but Jake can't believe she's chosen now to punish him, when everything came together so perfect, after the accidental serenade of those broken guitars. He pulls back her thumb like he's cocking a gun, hoping she'll flinch, asks again like a fool.

"What are you thinking?"

Still nothing.

...

Jake's uncle was on his sagging porch, fighting with a sticky switchblade, peeling apples so perfect they looked like cue balls.

"Are those even apples?" Cherry asked Jake as he kicked his car door shut and walked up the cinderblock steps, carrying her like a bride. He crushed a mosquito into a smear of war paint on her cheekbone without answering, then clucked his tongue and pretended to knock on an invisible door until his uncle looked up. Jake's uncle was blonde and big, just like Jake, but leathery, not quite like he'd been through a fire, more like he'd stood too close to them all his life.

"Hey, Jake!"

"Hey, Jake!"

Jake's Uncle Jake even wore the same red-and-blue Highland High jacket as his nephew, the dog-eared "HHS" hanging by a thread, holes worn in leather elbows faded almost pink. Jake dropped out a full year earlier than his uncle though.

"They look good, don't they!" Uncle Jake beamed, pushing the button on his blade, which was still jammed up with sugar.

"Almost too juicy," Cherry said. "Are they rotten?"

"You're rotten, Cherry," Jake whispered to her, as he gently set her on the swing and sat between them. His uncle studied her confused, ready to say a whole lot more, but got stuck on the name like Jake knew he would.

"What the fuck did you call her?" Uncle Jake asked him.

"Baby, this is my Uncle Jake," Jake wrapped one loving hand around her back to give her neck a squeeze.

"Not another one!" she laughed a little too loud. "This your namesake?"

"I guess."

"You ever seen *The Two Jakes*?" she asked them.

"Yeah, right here on my porch, numbnuts!" Uncle Jake answered, and Cherry snickered, having never been called that before.

"Oh, you think that's funny?" Then to Jake, "What did you call her? Don't even…"

"This is Cherry."

"Another Cherry Bomb, huh. Or is it C.B. for short?"

"Hey, it's a popular name," Jake shrugged.

"Mm-hmm. So you want to be confusing, eh?" Uncle Jake laughed, and Jake frowned.

"Where's your Cherry anyway?"

"In the garage."

"Garage? Well, I was hoping we could all talk about…"

"What are you guys whispering about?" Cherry asked, and Jake's hand stroked her neck to soothe away some questions. He suddenly had less control of her than he'd had that morning.

"So, what the fuck happened to you, kid!" Uncle Jake barked, some of his confusion giving way to understanding. He finally noticed the road rash across his nephew's face, "Where's your ride? Back to the El Diablo I see."

"Someone 'Jake Braked' him," Cherry said cheerfully. "Both of us, really."

"What the hell does that mean?"

"It means someone jammed a baseball bat in the spokes of his Harley," she went on. "Sent us flying."

"Well, it wasn't a baseball bat," Jake corrected.

"Never mind that," Uncle Jake said. "Is she telling me that's what they call it when someone jams something in your spokes? Jake Breaking? It happens that often, they named that shit?"

"Guess so," Jake laughed nervously. "Here's the thing. I was hoping I could raid your garage for—"

"No, not Jake Breaking. Like 'Jake Braking,'" Cherry interrupted, still eager to explain. "It's actually called 'Jacob Braking.' You know, engine braking? You get it installed on your diesel, and when it lets the air out of the cylinders, it slows down your truck. Saves your brakes, but it sounds like a little boy making a machine-gun noise with his lips. People in the 'burbs hate it, and—"

"I know what fucking Jake Braking is," Uncle Jake said, still looking at Jake. "The question is, why is that the name for getting dropped like a bitch?"

"Because when he hit the ground, it let the air out of him," Cherry said, voice low. "But mostly because his fucking name was Jake."

Now he was finally looking at her, so Jake took an apple from under his uncle's knife and took a big bite, eyebrow up. Turned out it was those damn kiwis again, back in season. He loved kiwis. Jake looked down between his feet and saw the green skins piled under the swing. His uncle kicked them out of sight in disgust.

...

She still won't talk to him, but there's something Jake is saving. A last resort. A kind of "Break Glass In Case Of Emergency" expedient he can no longer resist.

There's always been a strange muscle somewhere in Jake's head. He doesn't know what it does, or how he flexes it, but it's somewhere behind his eyes, or between his ears, perched above the hinge in his jaw. And when Jake squeezes something deep in there—like biting down, but more like biting with his brain—he hears this…rumble. Like holding a seashell up to his head when a train goes by. He's never told anyone, as his greatest fear is that it does nothing at all. His earliest disappointment as a boy, discovering the rumble between his ears didn't start fires or stop anyone's heart, was almost too much to bear. But as he got older, he thought maybe he could use the rumble to move things. He worked on real cars first, then toys. Then he tried it on the older boys, the ones with the best bikes who would smack him upside the head whenever he rode by on his Schwinn Stingray, faking motorcycle noises with his mouth. But he never crashed them either. Sometimes out of habit, he'd still make a wish, flex that muscle, and see if that could bring down a plane.

So tonight he doesn't need to ask the question. Tonight he's going to use the rumble to know exactly what Cherry's thinking. He's suddenly convinced this is what the rumble in his head was always meant for.

He forces her into the back seat. There's resistance when her legs go the wrong way. No words, but a squeak he translates as laughter. To him, this tiny, almost imperceptible scoff sounds something like a thousand rotten apples falling into helicopter blades, spraying endless pulp over his face as the planet laughs along with her. He almost gags.

Then he flexes the strange muscle in his head harder than he ever has, and it must be working this time, because the rumble transforms into the sound of her voice, and she can't help but tell him everything that's on her mind.

...

"Hey, Uncle Jake! Where's your other jacket? I wanted to show off your gang colors."

"Oh, shit," Uncle Jake said, stabbing his blade into the wooden arm to hold it. "You talking about Deuces Wild?" He leaned over to rub Cherry's knee. She didn't blink. "Our gang was supposed to be called 'Deuces Wild,' right? Only the bitch that sewed up our satin jackets for us can't spell, right, so we get 'Deuches Wild' instead. On all five of 'em. You know, Dooshes Wild?"

"Oh, no!" Cherry squealed.

"But here's the thing," Jake said. "His gang was so tough, they left it. How badass is that?"

"Yeah, right," Uncle Jake laughed. "Running around, calling ourselves douches before anyone else can, I guess that's a tactic. And big letters, too! Right under a couple of dice. Of course, the dice looked like boxes with air holes cut in 'em for catching fucking frogs. Cherry, it sounds like a joke, but we were tough, I swear. The girls went ape over a tough guy with a nice mix of stupid."

Jake laughed.

"We'd kill you," Uncle Jake said, all serious. "Well, not you, baby," he added as he rubbed Cherry's knee a little longer, trying and failing to tickle it. His nephew pulled her away.

"Go get the jacket, Uncle Jake. Please?"

"Nah, it's in the garage soaking up oil." He wrestled his blade loose again. "I'll bet some of those other mooks still wear their around though. Mine had 'Uck' sewn right here over the heart, right where this HHS is hanging. My gang name was 'Uncle Duck,' you see, which everyone twisted into 'Duncle Uck' when they got buzzed."

"Where'd that come from?" Cherry asked.

"My hair was more yellow back then, like your boy's there. And I had that duck's ass in the back, bigger and higher and badder than anyone. But nobody really called me 'Duck' too much, especially this motherfucker, huh, Jake? He wants to be me so bad, he can't stand it."

He punched his nephew harder than necessary, and the swing rattled and shook.

"Did everybody have a nickname, Uncle Jake?" she asked.

"I ain't your uncle, girl! Hell, I'm not his either. I'm his Uncle Uncle Jake if you want to get technical. Great Uncle or some shit. But they never proved it."

In the distance, someone rolled down their window to sing along with the Stones.

"*I see the girls walk by dressed in their summer clothes…I have to turn my head until my darkness goes…*"

Cherry turned red, and Uncle Jake put his foot down to stop the swing. "She looks just like her, you know?"

...

The rumble of her voice fills his ears to the brim. Finally, everything she's thinking, rolling like thunderheads…

I don't know why he's looking at me like I'm scared. My first time wasn't scary. And it sure wasn't him. And it got real easy once I knew I didn't have to get naked. All you need is one leg out of your jeans. God damn, why do they try so hard to scare us…

Jake kicks off one of her shoes and works her pink leg out into the night, her joints are loose, her skin smooth as bone. She's limp, but her voice is getting louder.

It doesn't mean anything if I've done it before. Does he get this?

Her voice echoing, Jake tries digging his fingernails into her leg, scratching for a grip through his own sweat. He sees the half-moons he'll leave behind when a nail flips back.

Why's he trying to steer me by my pelvis? Did he get that from Elvis? His fingers are fucked from smashing too many guitars.

Jake buries a thumb between her legs, searching for heat and finding none, using it to pull her higher. His movements are abrupt, petulant. The resistance mocks him, and now the crickets are drowning out her voice. Even his rumble.

How many crickets are there in the world? Don't know. I read somewhere if they rub their legs together hard enough, they can catch fire. They have to jump to flame-out. That's how you get lightning bugs...

Jake can't believe she's heard the same ridiculous story about fireflies, something he made up as a boy, and he tries harder to get a better grip. But it's hard, she's hard, and his wet fingers keep slipping off the handles of her bone, pitching him forward and off balance. He locks an arm under her throat before she can laugh again and in desperation tries to work all his fingers inside her. Up to his wrist, he watches her black eyes for a reaction. He swears he gets a splinter.

...

"Let me tell you the best advice I ever heard, boy. Hold your nose and eat a spider first thing in the morning and nothing worse will happen to you all day."

"You said that before, Uncle Jake. But I thought it was a frog."

"What's the difference?"

"The amount of chewing, for one." He started rocking again, staring at the girl, her unblinking eyes and her glassy, almost translucent skin, slick as a Coke bottle in the sun. He followed her blood-red hair down the middle of her back, the blood you'd find in movies, too bright to be real. She was colors not found in nature.

"Uncle Jake..."

"Do me a favor. Just call me 'Jake.' The two-uncle thing just ruined it forever."

"Okay, but it's gonna get weird," Jake shrugged.

"You know what, boy? Your Cherry reminds me of my Cherry. That's no accident, is it?"

"Well, there was an accident actually—"

"You had a Cherry, too?" she asked, as Jake twirled hair behind her ears.

"Sure did! But my Cherry was a little different. She had this game she liked to play."

"What game is that?" Cherry sounded worried about where the story was going, but Jake just smiled and mimed like he was buckling a seat belt for a good yarn.

"It was called Dead Girl On The Side Of The Road."

"Whoa."

"I know, right!" Both Jakes stomped their feet. "Wanna try it?"

"Uh, no?"

"Aw, come on! You kids don't know fun if it bit ya. It was a gas. My Cherry swore she made it up, too. Here's how it went down. First, she'd make me take her out for Chinese food to go. Sweet 'n' sour pork. Them Orientals were only a decade out of the camps, so they were working their asses off, even outside of Chinatowns, so we'd get plenty of rice. But we'd get an extra order just in case. White rice. Not that brown healthy shit. Then we'd drive out to a dead-end road off a dead-end road and drop her off with the grub. Then I'd come back a little later, playing like I'm just driving along, right? And she'd be lying there, waiting."

"I thought it was Japan in those camps," Jake muttered.

"Was she playing possum?" Cherry asked.

"Ha, more like playing pussy!" Uncle Jake laughed. "She's lying there, and she's got rice and noodles sprinkled all over her body, corners of her mouth, her ears, eyes, between her legs…" He felt the two scooting away and stopped. "What? You know, like maggots and worms! More rice than newlyweds running from a church. Come on, keep up. So I come across her lying there, and I pretend I find a dead girl on the side of the road, you dig?"

"So, then what?" Cherry asked, not really wanting to know.

"Then I brush off the rice and fuck her! What do you think? I'm telling you, that shit's better than a honeymoon."

The two of them shook their heads as he picked up speed.

"No, no, I ain't done. I ain't done. So, the last time we do this, I'm working to get her jeans off, but her knees were locked tight, right? You punks today and your tight asses had nothing on a Teddy Girl in the 50's. You'd need your blade to get her out, to tell you the truth. And normally I probably woulda used one. But here it worked with the game, because it was like rigor mortis, you get it? But at that moment, since she's so stiff, I'm also thinking she's changed her mind, like I'd waited too long to come back and she had time to think how ridiculous it all was."

"Can you blame her?"

"Listen, when she wanted to, her legs would lock so tight you could hear them humming like an oncoming train. So I started whispering to her. Pillow talk. First just told her to snap out of it, please baby, baby, but then I started telling her other stuff, too. Pleading for real, even some weird sincere shit. Then I don't know what happened because her finger is suddenly jabbing me in the ribs, looking at me all strange, but with love, you know, too much love for a crazy girl who just smeared Jap food all over herself."

"Wait, so what are you—"

"We'd fallen asleep, I guess. She was asleep before I got back. But then I crashed there, too. And when we checked our watches, it was actually earlier than when we'd started."

"I don't get it."

"We slept there on the side of the road until the next day! Dead? Alive? I don't know. Shit gets weird on the road. I just know we spent 24 hours together in a ditch with rice on our faces like a couple of open assholes."

"You know what we did?" Cherry said, sitting up straight. "We made snow angels in a ditch once! Well, dirt angels. There's a reason they do it in snow, you know. Got our elbows all bloody, like this..."

"Shut up," Uncle Jake said, looking around for his knife. "I'll tell ya though, the side of a road is more comfortable than you think. Don't jump to conclusions if you see a dead body. Might just be a catnap."

Jake glared for a second, mad at how he talked to Cherry. But the sun was going down, and his Uncle Jake was one of those guys who smoothed out once the sun went down.

"Where did you meet her?" Cherry asked him.

"A bar! Where else?"

"What were you doing?"

"Playing pool? Playing fool? What else was there back then?" he laughed. "It was at The Bone Yard, so the pool table was jacked, of course. About as level as my balls in a hundred-degree weather. Hey, I stole their sign once. Everybody stole their signs to hang 'em over their bed. Drove Ray nuts. But Ray stole my sign right back for his own bed. Remember my music store? The Cherry Tree? Any guitar your heart desired. Electric or neutered. Les Paul, Neubauer, Albanus, Gibson, Radio Tone, Fender, Alamo. Remember the Alamos?! Still got a pile of broken Radio Tones in the back..."

"The Cherry Tree!" Cherry laughed. "No way."

"Would George Washington lie about a name like that?"

"The Bone Yard, huh? I've heard of that place. Isn't that where Gay Busted Elvis hangs out?"

"Yep! One and the same. Except back then, we called him High-Strung Elvis. He was just this big plaster Elvis bust someone glued rainbows of string all over for hair. Only later, like the '70s and '80s, did people start calling him 'Pride Elvis' or 'Rainbow Elvis' or whatever, which is what led directly to him being called 'busted.' Have you seen his face lately? Cracked right down the middle, so he's only half-a-fag now. Two thirds at best. Well, they'd have to weigh him. You've been there, right, Jake? But back then, The Bone Yard was like most dives, every goof in there trying to imitate some Limey Café hangout in the movies with their flitty Café Racers. All day long, every one of 'em bullshittin' about bench-racing imaginary cars, every one of 'em a photo finish. Except instead of Frankie Limey and The Fuckin' Teenagers' 'Why Do Fools Fall In Love?' on the jukebox, it was all Elvis, all the time. And all his goddamn songs were questions, too. Those were the worst! 'How's The World Treating You?' 'How Do You Think I Feel?' 'What The Fuck Are You Thinking?' My favorite from '56 was always 'Paralyzed'..."

"What was wrong with the pool table?"

"It had an extra hole, for starters. Right in the middle where balls would go airborne on the break. Someone tried to fix it by filling it with tree sap, but that just made it worse. The night I met Cherry, I'd been slinging hash with these guys, buncha candy asses claiming to be Stone Grease outta Chicago, and they were swearing up and down that the hole in the table was really a bullet hole. And it was working, impressing these twits at the bar. So I jumped into the story, too, trying to help a brother out. Now, I wasn't as good with stories back then as I am now, so I just said, 'Yeah, they're right! There was this fight, and the punk who lost came marching back in at close like Stagger Lee, right past the guys that beat his ass—not regulars either, Big Four or at least associates—but instead of lighting them up, or popping the bottles behind the bar or the fins off the ceiling fan or any of that shit you're supposed to do in a story like this, he just walked up to the pool table, put his snub-nose flush against the green and BAM!' Well, the debs were impressed as all hell with my story, and they kept feeding the table quarters all night to play these dudes, so they finally got drunk and their game started to slip enough for me to start betting. Then Cherry comes walking in. She's wearing a red T-shirt and jeans, or cherry stains all over them or something, crisp blues way too big—the only time I ever seen 'em that way—and rolled up to her knees. And she points at the hole in the pool table and proceeds to blow my whole story out of the water with a story of her own. It would have been okay if she'd just told her fable and that was that, but hers was much better than mine. Plus she acted it out in a way I never coulda topped."

"I've heard this!" Jake shouted.

"You might have. It's like this loony barfly variation on 'The Princess And The Pea' she starts doing. First, she jumps up on the pool table and lays back, eyes closed, then she tries to guess what balls everybody's knocking into the holes—get this—by just the feel of them under her body. She does this awhile, us banging away, her maybe getting her guesses right, maybe not, but it doesn't fuckin' matter with those white knees high up in the sky like that, and all us assholes are drooling on her, and then she starts fingering that hole like it's a real asshole and telling us how she's only in there looking to buy fireworks from Ray the bartender and how he shorted her last time. See, fireworks were like bullets back then. Meaning they were everywhere…"

"I thought she told a story."

"I was getting to that. Fuck. Let me think. Okay, so, laying there on her back, she tells us all that she played this 'Princess And The Pea' action in The Bone Yard once before, but someone tried to trick her by taking one of Ray's M-80's or whatever out of the back, and then dropping it down the corner pocket after the 8-ball when she wasn't looking. Rattle rattle rattle rattle…BOOM! Something like that. Wait, it wasn't an M-80. It was a cherry bomb. Of course it was a cherry bomb! But really, my story was better, only I don't have the knees for it. Oh, shit, and when she pulled up the back of her shirt to show us a scar on the sweet spot of her spine from the cherry bomb—well, fuck it—game over. No one even remembered I was talking. Except for Rusty."

"Oh, no. Not Rusty." Jake knew all about Rusty. The enemy of every biker with chrome between his legs was a Rusty.

"Yeah. See, there was this other guy, Rusty Games, who was always eating big red apples all sloppy all over the pool sticks. His dad had an orchard, see? He got that nickname for being terrible at 8-ball, but sometimes we just called him 'Games.' Or even 'Rusty Names.' Hey, at least we didn't call him 'Rusty Dames,' I guess. Anyway, Rusty Games puts 'Walk Fuck Like A Man' on the jukebox—"

"Wait, what song?" Cherry asked.

"You never heard that?"

"I think you're mixing up two songs there, Uncle Jake."

"You're nuts. But Games, he was a goddamn storyteller. Told wicked stories all the time. The one I remember best he told us that night. How he stole his daddy's Buddy Holly album and hid it in his own stack. And his stack was up to your neck, right? Most people only had 45's, so that was a red flag right there. But Games says his daddy's threatening to tip 'em over, and he says his daddy says he better dig it out careful if he knows what's good for him. Now, going through a stack like that to find one record is no easy task. That's heavy. By 'heavy,' I mean heavy, like real work. So his daddy pulls a fucking gun and says, 'Boy, you gimmie my *Chirping Crickets* el peeeee!' and Games says he says, 'Fuck you!' and snatches his daddy's .45..."

"The record or the gun?"

"...the gun, not the record. Swipes it right out of his hand, goes over to this leaning tower of pizza and says, 'Pick a card! Any card!' Which I guess was his way of saying, 'Guess how many records the bullet goes through,' right? And Games says his daddy's worried now because *The Chirping Crickets* by Buddy Holly and The Motherfucking Crickets is probably near the top of the stack. But it's too late. Games puts that gun in the middle of the stack and fires straight down. *BLAM!* Turns out he shoots right through the doughnut holes! Swore he didn't scratch a single record. Or kill a single cricket. Didn't send anything flying except maybe the songs themselves. So, after this story, Cherry's all in love. So I clear my throat and say, 'Bullshit!' And that's when Games punches me in the mouth."

"Oh, man. We know a fucker like that, too, don't we, baby?" Jake said, petting her head. "Except he punched my bike in the mouth. Did he ride a little dirt bike like a bear on a unicycle?" But Jake knew he didn't. He knew Games had heavy metal just like him and his uncle. Jake knew all about Games. Uncle Jake practically raised Jake after his dad died, and he talked about Games a lot. So he knew how this story ended, but the stories in the middle always changed.

"So I sat pouting, rubbing my face and listening to him tell more stories. After that punch, everyone was listening really."

"Did you guys rumble?" Cherry asked, and Jake's hand squeezed the back of her neck tighter than normal to quiet her down.

"Don't say 'rumble,' baby. In this family, it doesn't mean what you think it does."

"Both of you, zip it. So my heartbeat's in my lips, but I'm still in ear-shot when Games starts laying it on thick, sniffing her neck, nuzzling and telling her stories like this one about two cats that used to fuck under the hood of his Mustang when he was a kid. The way he tells it, you'd think it was a sonnet. He whispers to her how he heard these alien sounds in his car, followed them to their source, and his daddy said, 'Don't look under there!' Said it was probably just a brain-damaged cat licking antifreeze. But Games says he was so sure it was the ghosts of roadkill that he has to look, baby…" He nuzzled up to Cherry's cold neck, and she didn't flinch. "…but all he saw were the tails, he tells her. But that's enough. Three Elvis songs later, they're holding hands. Another song later, they're holding even more. But I watch him close all night. I knew he had a blade by the outline in his back pocket. Knew he'd cut someone recently by the wet stain around it. He played the part, you know? Had the Jesus boots like me, like you, like all of us back then. But just like us, this motherfucker had to piss eventu-ally, and that's where I decided I'd get back on his radar."

…

Still ain't working, is it, Jake? You remind me of that joke. Boy sticks in a finger. Girl says, "One more." Boy sticks in another finger. Girl says, "One more." Boy sticks in all his fingers. Girl says, "More!" Boy sticks in his whole hand. Girl says, "Stick in your other hand, too." Boy sticks in both hands. Girl says, "Clap your hands." Boy says, "I can't." Girl says, all smug, "Tight, ain't it?"

Jake loses sight of the numbers on his watch while Cherry's feet violently drum the window over his shoulder from his effort. When it shatters, Jake sighs.

Those aren't so easy to come by on a Cadillac, he thinks. It was hard enough finding a new door after I opened it on that kid's face.

Jake's car is streaked with gray primer from the door handles on up, so he calls it his Great White Shark. Tonight, with the windshield busted, he imag-ines it swimming around upside down, mouth wide open.

No room in here, Jake. You know, I saw a girl in a stag movie once, one of the nasty ones, say she fucks hundreds every year, but saves her ass for whoever she loves. There's a moral there somewhere.

Jake puts more weight on the arm across her throat and pulls his hand out far enough to see the numbers on his Eterna Automatic. He was sure having it inside her would make it stop from more heat and pressure than any timepiece was built to endure. He thinks about the clocks that stopped when they tested the atom bomb. He thinks sun-dials the size of football fields and the thunderclouds that render them useless. Then he goes in deeper.

I don't know why you think you can do any damage. You'd have to fuck me with something bigger than a fist, bigger than a baby, bigger than a baby riding a motorcycle...

Jake tries to think of things babies do and decides fingernails are the answer. Babies never scratch anything but themselves or they'd scratch their way out. He wonders what keeps kittens from escaping their mothers' bellies. Her voice in his head is loud but bored, a lethal combination.

You'll never be half the man my daddy was. When I had my first exam, the doctor waited and wasted time until daddy was back in the room and next to me, then he asked if I was a virgin. Bastard's fingers just discovered I wasn't, you know? He thought daddy would be angry. And he was. But not at me. Daddy climbed over a model of diseased ovaries on the desk and punched that motherfucker so hard his hand disappeared. Then he took me home. That punch was so loud, sometimes I feel I could ride it like a saddle.

Jake starts scratching and digging like a kitten, trying to find something inside her no one has before. And he does. Something small and hard. He traces its outline, squeezes rubber that feels like a wheel. He hopes it's not a toy, and his fingers curl tight to wrestle it out. He imagines chains and bubbles and the groan of an engine as a car is slowly dragged from a swamp.

Too bad I never saw that doctor again because my daddy wanted to stick something in there to surprise him next time. Give him the surprise of his life. There never was a next time, but it was a good idea. Almost as good as this one...

That's when Cherry twists her hips so hard and fast that his middle finger cracks at the second knuckle. He pulls out, a silent scream circling his mouth, a knee in her neck to keep her down as he feels around in the dark to trace the new trajectory of his digit. He counts two extra knuckles he didn't have before and splintered bone rolling under the skin. It reminds him of the stone in his elbow from the last time he got dumped off his bike riding a corn maze.

Serves you right, Jake. My teeth are clenched, yes, but it's just the way I'm made. It's not the silent treatment, I swear. Hang it up.

Jake uses the heel of his injured hand for leverage and tries again, rotating his shoulder for power. He remembers playing doctor when he was a boy, and a girl on the playground asked him to unwrap his apple then wrap that aluminum foil around his finger to stick it down her throat. They thought it would make his finger a mirror so they could see deep inside her body. This memory has always haunted him. Especially when she threw up and he fought to keep that silver finger inside to find her heart. That's how you played doctor for real.

Then his finger finds the trigger and her mouth finally blows open to let out the smoke.

...

"If you've been to The Bone Yard for longer than three beers, then you know the toilets are always broken. And Ray the bartender—sorry son-of-a-bitch never rode a bike that wasn't crop-dusting with a blown rod—he'd play this crazy game where he'd put Siamese fighting fish in 'em to see how long they'd last, as a joke."

"Never heard that joke."

"You never heard that joke? Doctor says he needs a blood, urine, semen, and fecal sample so the patient hands him his underwear? Well, that's the toilets in The Bone Yard in a nutshell. But those fighting fish? Sometimes they wouldn't die. Ray's funny like that. He also likes to roll his quarters on the bar when he cleans out the machines, something dumbasses like me used to think were dangerous as brass knuckles. So while I'm standing there twirling my church key and killing time, not ready to pop the top on another Coca-Cola because someone will swipe it when our fight starts, I palm a roll of Ray's quarters and keep them close. Then finally Games struts in there to piss. I move fast. I'd already put the loudest song on the jukebox in case he screamed—I had a long time to think about it with his endless stories. So I walk right in behind him, and I punch him over the ear, and the paper breaks and quarters explode everywhere. But it's enough of a shock for me to get both his arms locked behind his back before he knows what the hell is going on. He doesn't yell out. Instead he uses all his strength to get one arm free. Then, at the last possible second—you gotta picture this shit. I'm pushing his head towards that black water in slow-motion, where a Siamese fighting fish is fighting a turd or worse—and right before the tip of his nose is gonna go *sploosh!* he reaches up and catches the chain to flush that bitch."

"Chain?"

"It was a different time. Everything had chains back then, not just us."

"But you said these toilets don't flush."

"That's what I thought! Turned out they worked fine. Just no one ever flushed 'em!"

"He didn't get dunked? Aw, man! He beat you again."

"You don't know the half of it. Story ain't over. So his face slaps the bowl, and it's nasty, but not as nasty as that black mud aquarium. But I'm so surprised it flushed that he gets the best of me, and after some slap-happy rabbit punches and slipping around on quarters, suddenly I'm over another bowl that's even worse, one where the Rumble Fish is floating and never had a fucking chance at all, and now I'm heading for the dunk of the damned. But he's only got one of my arms, just like I had on him, and I go for the chain, too, because I'm a quick study. And…I catch it at the last second like I'm going off a fuckin' cliff."

"Whew! Close one, Uncle Jake."

"Close one, my ass. Imagine this. Freeze the scene with my face in the same spot his was. Then move your camera up the toilet a bit. See that box? Inside that box, the chain goes down, and this little metal bar goes up, and there's another little chain, see? A little chain that Games cut earlier that evening with his switchblade. And when I pull my chain, it only makes this little chain swirl around a bit, barely even tickling the rubber plug that would have been my savior. All that clear, cold water in the box could have saved me from a mouthful of shit, piss, blood and dead fish, and quarters."

"Man, he must be psychic. How do you know that he cut it?" Jake asked.

"The stains on his back pocket. That's why his blade was wet."

"Come on now, how would he know to do that? How did he know what you were going to do? How would he know which toilet to pick?" Cherry wanted to know.

"The one with the fish, of course. He knew I'd aim for the fish that was still fighting, and that left the toilet with the dead one."

"I guess. But why would he—"

"Hey! You think I'm pulling your chain?" Big smirk. Then, "Listen! You ever seen those little flies they paint on urinals nowadays? It reduces piss stains by a thousand percent. It's our lizard brain—we can't help but aim for living things."

"Girls don't use urinals."

"Not your best idea following him in there, huh, Uncle Jake?"

"Not my worst idea either. I'll tell you about that one sometime—when me and your dad tried to make a haunted house out of your Grandpa Jake's garage."

"So how'd you end up with her?" Cherry needed to know.

"Huh? My bike?"

"No. Your Cherry. If Games got the best of you, how'd you end up with her?"

"End up with her. It's funny you say it like that."

...

Jake drives around in his shark, wind drying his eyes, taking a twisted route so the sun is always coming up behind him. He tries not to look at his bent, throbbing finger, a bloody maraschino topping his wheel. After a couple miles, he finds a boy on a bicycle, a Stingray just like his, and he cruises behind with the muscle rumbling loud in his ear. It's not a dirt bike, but it'll have to do because it's the boy's voice he hears now.

What the hell is he doing up so early?

The boy glances back at the shark and kicks his heel down on a generator connected to his back tire. Jake sees a tiny wheel snap down on the white wall and red tail-light on the bike's fender growing steadily brighter. Jake realizes the boy is pretending he's fired up some sort of engine, imagining his tiny tail-light is some kind of rocket. Jake gets closer and sees cards in the spokes, not playing cards but some goddamn role-playing game with dragons instead of hearts, and now Jake is furious. This is even worse than a dirt bike and has no business on his road. But it's still just a kid. So he reaches back behind his seat and plucks ammo from his 8-ball collection racked in a triangle, pool balls he'd stolen mid-game to impress Cherry during their courtship. He'd steal a ball and get chased out the door, then steal a kiss from her behind the dumpster. He had 8-balls rolling free around his shark until one rolled under his brake pedal and he couldn't stop without almost doing a headstand. He took out five mailboxes that day, but it could have been worse. And they worked a lot better than his piles of vinyl .45s he used like exploding Frisbees when someone wanted to race at a red light. Perfect for situations like this.

He used to collect the 8-balls with the water in them, the toys that told you what you were thinking. He even had one on his dashboard for a while, but half its guts evaporated in the sunlight, leaving the die stuck with just one answer on the window, "Concentrate And Ask Again." He tried taking this advice, but it ruined him and his girl forever. Even with a bullet finally blowing her mouth open for good, he knew she'd never talk again. Not just because of what he stole from her.

...

"How did I end up with her? Well, me and Games decided we'd have to earn her. So we agreed on a story. We agreed on a time. We agreed on a road…"

"For a rumble!"

"I told you not to say that word," Jake said, rubbing his head.

"For a race?" Cherry asked, sheepish.

"No, no, no. I told him I'll be with Cherry in my car, romancing her best I can. I'll try to tell her a ghost story, you know? Get her to believe it. He had this key ring for his bike made out of a green apple—no, a kiwi—with a little plastic sword sticking out—he said it came off some weird drink Ray made for him—and he called this thing his "Martian Pussy." And it really looked like something he'd been fucking, right, even though he swore he wasn't going to fuck it until it turned brown—"

"What kind of bike did he ride?"

"Oh, he rode one of those dustbin fairies, a Moto Guzzi. Into that new streamliner shit. So, he gives me the 'Martian Pussy' for bad luck, and we chose our roles. He decided he'd be the ghost and I'd be the ghost story. And may the best man win!"

"I don't get it."

"I'd rather be the ghost."

"It goes like this: I'd take Cherry down Mantis Trail in my car, right around the bridge where we'd watch submarine races…"

"What car?"

"You know what car, Jake! The same two-tone shitbox I gave to you!"

"Ha! Submarine races!" Cherry squealed. "I know what those were."

"That ain't slang, girl. Naw, up by Mantis Trail was this big delta with an Army base about six miles up so we could see real submarines on test runs. Wait, what did you think it meant? Fuck it. Anyhow, yeah, the bridge, that's where I'd start the story. Games would be doing about 90 per, since he's the ghost and all, then I'd reach a point in the yarn where I'd stop cold, take the Martian Pussy from the ignition and throw the keys off into the creek. Not my keys, but she doesn't know that. I'd have an extra key for later, tucked under the saddle of my bike. Then, when I've locked us out, or she thinks I've locked us out…"

"How are you locked out?" Cherry asked. "Now you're on a bike? You just said your saddle—"

"Without keys, you're locked out in the dark. Get it? So she'll be scared, thinking we're stuck. And right about then, I'd get to the part of the ghost story with a phantom bike or some shit, I don't remember exactly…"

Uncle Jake stopped to lean over and squint into a spider web on the rail. A grasshopper was struggling mightily, and its panic caught his eye the same time as the wolf spider living in his tunnel. But Uncle Jake moved quicker than the spider, quicker than Jake thought possible, and plucked it out first. The grasshopper puked on his finger, and he crushed it in disgust.

"Where was I?"

"A phantom bike or some shit," Cherry said.

"Right."

"What kind of bike did you have?" she needed to know.

"I have a hog! Same as yours. I mean, his. You know that. Orange and black. Called it my Halloween 'Sickle.'"

"Sickle, like 'motor-sickle'?"

"No, you know, a sickle. Like the Reaper carries."

"Ah."

"Harley '56 HK, a bobber by accident right now, but the same bike Elvis posed on that very same year for the cover of May's *Enthusiast*. Yeah, it's a 'Hardly Ableson,' the only thing they allowed up in Sturgis or the Black Hills. Thirteen-forty see-sees, two-valve vee-twin, swing-arm pipes so you don't go gunnin' it without watching those corners. Otherwise you'll drop your pumpkins, Ichabod-style…"

"What?"

"You can't throw a pumpkin if you don't have a good center of gravity!" He patted his beer belly hard, laughing. "So. Ghost story. We're standing on the bridge, just talking. It wasn't dark enough yet, and it was a hot night, one of those steamy ones. And that's when the fog broke, and we saw this boy on the water, frozen in a dive, hovering above the surface."

"What do you mean 'frozen'?"

"Frozen. Like a snapshot. It was this kid, caught coming off a diving board, stopped just above the water a split second before his hands would have pierced the waves. First, I thought it was just some boy surfing a submarine. But as he floated closer, I couldn't get my brains around it. He was too far out in the river to have jumped from anywhere but the motherfucking sky. So we're staring as he moves with the current, still locked in this crazy dive. Then the boy's legs start twitching, then scissoring, then pedaling the air. I thought I was losing my mind for sure. Still up and down arrow-straight, he's moving towards us while his legs pin-wheel, his fingers spread like he was stretching the surface tension, looking for a way in. I'm wanting to punch myself in the mouth to wake up from this dream, when the fog finally breaks and give us a clear view. I can see the boy's hands, see hands fanned out, and I finally understand, and my heartbeat returns to normal. He's on a raft. It was just a boy doing a headstand on a raft. I didn't realize it then, but now I know that he's the reason it all went wrong that night. After seeing something like that, with no words needed to paint the picture, there was just no way any story that came out of my mouth would compete."

...

The last time Jake was on this road, he was under it. He had crawled into a drainage tunnel near the railroad tracks because he was in love with a girl but didn't have the nerve to tell her. So he spray-painted "Ask me what I'm thinking" on the wall of the tunnel and took her to find it. When they were creeping towards it, flashlight bobbing around like an erection, so proud of his surprise, a train thundered over them and she started backing out. He got angry and told her there was something she had to see. But she didn't care. She was scared of the noise, then scared of him. So he started to lie, claimed there was a strange opening in the wall, some nonsense about miles and miles of mysterious tunnels leading into the dark. He thought she'd need to see that, but it only scared her more. She was running down the tracks back to his Stingray before he could even back out. He stood in the rumble of the train, and he knew what she was thinking. They rode home in silence, and nothing could get her back down there. Not even when he hooked her antenna with a 45 while she was idling at a stop sign. And when he finally did say those three words, they meant nothing at all.

Jake taps the gas pedal, flashes his brights, then flips the switch on the heater, imagining he's triggered a ragged chum-dripping mouth under the grill to scoop up his upcoming roadkill. His shark drifts over the double-yellow, sniffing for blood. Then Jake leans out his window, thinks something like, "Outlook Not So Good," and side-arms an 8-ball into the boy's spokes.

The fantasy cards flutter in the rooster tail of rocks as the boy squeezes his front brakes and flies headfirst over his handle bars. The bike chases his tumble into the ditch, greased chain still clicking smooth when they land. Jake backs up to see where the boy vanished, hissing through his teeth when he pulls the gearshift too tight and a greenstick fracture splits through his skin. The shark dances backwards on the rumble strip, then skids in the gravel as Jake pops the passenger door and shadows his crime. Jake looks down into the ditch for about ten seconds, then grabs the .45—the gun not the record—that still rests between Cherry's legs where it was born. He puts one bullet in the boy's head, then another in his mouth just in case, then stabs the gas and goes hand-over-hand on the steering wheel to spin around and leave the ditch behind. When the shark straightens out, he wrings out his wheel like laundry and sucks his broken finger some more. It's changing colors again, and he remembers the first time he ever buried it in a real, live girl back in sixth grade and how scared he was when he saw it turn green under the glow of the dashboard lights.

Then the sun is coming around to face him again, and it hurts to turn and stay ahead. The roads will be filling up soon, and suddenly he knows what everyone will be thinking. Without squeezing the muscle in his head. He adjusts his radio, but the rumbles grow louder.

• • •

"Because I'm so caught up in the game, she starts telling me her own ghost story first! And now I know I'm fucked. She goes, 'Picture it, you're driving down the road…' She's saying this while she's flicking thorns at my face, right, long, crabapple thorns from Games' orchard that stung like a mother, so I'm turning away, and she grabs—"

"What kind of orchard grows crabapples?"

"That's what I'm saying. Him and his brothers had a cornfield that grew nothing but dirt-bike rallies, too. Anyhow, she grabs my jaw to straighten my head and goes, 'Okay, you're driving down the road…' Then, nose to nose, she puts one finger on a nostril and blows snot in my face. I jump up with, 'What the fuck?!' and she laughs and says, 'Bugs on your windshield. Pay attention, you're driving down the road…' And at that point, I just let her do what she wants to do, thinking it's all downhill after the bugs, but now she starts holding up her palms and taking long karate chops past my ears. 'Oncoming cars,' she tells me. Whoosh, whoosh, whoosh, her hands flying by my head. 'You're driving down the road…' she keeps saying, then, 'Now close your eyes.' And that's when she punches me in the mouth just like fucking Games. 'Never close your eyes when you're driving down the road,' she shrugs, smiling while blood drips off my bottom lip again like a fuckin' schoolboy."

"Sounds like a handful, Uncle Jake."

"Every time I took her riding on my hog, she wanted to switch places."

"You were just afraid to be seen in the bitch seat."

"Humbugs! Nothing wrong with that. Lines you up perfect, like doing it 'donkey style.'"

"Don't you mean 'doggy style'?"

"I mean what I mean. Donkey style. Now, let me ask you kids a question, mostly you, Jake. And your answer means everything. What's worst? Fucking a dead dog on the side of the road…or lying about it?"

"Uh…"

"Don't answer yet."

"Can I not answer ever?" Cherry said.

"Okay, back to that night. She tries another story on me, going, 'Picture this, you're running through the river…' and she's got this beer bottle she snagged from the side of the bridge that's full of foam and mosquito eggs and spunk-water—stanky shit, rank, we're talking upper ranks, rank of First Lieutenant at least—and she's shaking it up with her thumb over the spout, getting ready to splash me, and I go, 'Whoa, whoa, whoa. I'm not running through the river. My turn.' She says, 'Fine,' so all spooky, I say, 'It was a year ago tonight. And you're running through the woods…' And I start punching the air near her ears. She smiles, thinking no way I'm gonna hit her, right? 'You're running through the woods,' I say, swinging fists past her head, zip, zip zip."

The swing tilted as Uncle Jake reached around to get closer to his nephew and chop the air past his ears.

"You're running through the woods, Jake. Zip, zip, zip. That's what I tell her. Then I'm all like, 'Close your eyes.' You heard me, close 'em!" he yelled.

Jake closed his eyes and his uncle heeled him in the forehead with a sound like a steak dropped on a countertop.

"No way you hit a girl," Jake sighed, hand cupped over his eyes like he was saluting a lower rank.

"Says you," Uncle Jake scoffed. "Had to get her attention. 'It was a year ago tonight,' I was saying. That's how every ghost story starts. Then I switched to 'It was a week ago tonight,' thinking it would be scarier, but it just sounded dumb. So I take a jar out of my saddlebag, and I set it down on my front fender in front of the headlight, 'cause beforehand me and Games had filled it up with apple and kiwis, get me? Apples on the top, kiwis on the bottom. Red light, green light, got it? So if I click my high beams, it gives him a red light, meaning the scare is off. Too dangerous."

"Wait a second," Cherry said. "What's dangerous. And why the colors?"

"In case he blinks. I don't know. Didn't wanna take any chances. We can see red and green from miles away."

"How do you know green to him is green to you?" Cherry asked and got a heel to her forehead in return. Her head went back so far the two Jakes were surprised it came back.

"So I try my ghost story, some B.S. about a kid killing his best friend over a girl. Nothing new. Some horse hockey about a headless motorcycle rider like Sleep Hollow or something. But she interrupts me with her own story again. This one is about a horse, and it's fucking better than mine. Again."

"You're just not a storyteller, Uncle Jake."

"Guess not. Unless I'm telling stories about other people's stories. Anyhow, she tells me she was 6 or 7, on her uncle's ranch, obsessed with their horse named Serendipity—Sir, for short—and, oops, now 'Sir' is giving birth. She says she remembers the sucking sounds because it's the day the crickets stopped and she can hear everything, from both ends of the barn and both ends of the horse. Sir kicks up some dust, and Cherry tries her hardest not to look at the tunnel under her tail. Eventually, she closes her eyes and makes a wish, she tells me. She says she wishes the little horse that comes out of that hole will look like the horses she used to draw, like all little girls used to draw when we we're drawing motorcycles. She wishes for a centaur or a Pegasus, one with a man's head or one with wings. Either will do. Then the worst thing happens. Her wish comes true."

Jake never heard this story before, and he had one eye shut as if expecting another blow.

"The thing that came out of that hole haunted every farmhand to his grave. One rancher tried to pull her away. One cocked a shotgun while her father was pulling the thing out from under the whiplashing tail, one hand in front of his face like he's warding off the worst news in the world. She said there was this sudden blast of fluid, and that's when she sees the whole thing for the first time. It was deformed, of course, but to Cherry she just saw this shriveled snout, almost like a pig under glass, and a bunch of afterbirth stuck to its back that Sir is now hell-bent on eating. It's not just afterbirth she's munching though. Most of its insides were suddenly on the outside, and with every bite, the foal was screaming. The sac was coiled, and wet, wrapped around its ribs, and Cherry tells me that, in her young mind, she was sure this was wings. Like a bug slipping from a cocoon, wings straining to unfold. She was sure she got her horrible wish, and now Sir is chewing wings right off its back. She's convinced she caused this, suddenly sure this is what it looks like if a goddamned flying horse really happened. It wouldn't be something beautiful. It would be horror. She tells me how she watched Sir tugging on the back of the howling foal, ripping away the wings, and how all the men were screaming like children. Two shotgun blasts finally stopped everything, but not before she said she saw that foal standing up strong, soaking up buckshot like it was nothing, and spreading the rest of those tattered wings wide. She swore she saw huge wings beat dust and spider webs off the walls—and not the kind of noble wings you'd see on a drawing of some mythical creature, more like something you'd see on an insect, blue-veined like our balls, the wings of a fly drowning in your drink. Then she asks me, 'So, what were you saying then?'"

"Wow," Cherry said.

"Speak for your own balls," Jake said.

"Ha, we all got the same balls, boy. On a hot day like this, they all hang the same, like a plastic bag of guppies you buy to feed your fucking turtle. Swinging low and sloshing, trying not to touch your body to keep fighting fish from boiling."

"Ew."

"So this is what happened. I get so caught up in her story about the horse, her whispering that shit in my ear, head against my back, that I take my thumb off the brights. Her hand comes around to work me and my zipper, but I shake it away. No way I'm in the mood now. See, I was gonna give Games the red light no matter what, I really was. He'd stop the bike right before he went under the bridge, right before his neck got to the spot where I'd strung up the wire. A line of guitar string from my brother, your dad's Stratocaster, or maybe it was grandpa's piano— whatever's stronger—and Games would look at that wire and know he almost ended up with half a face. They'd both know what I almost did. But you know the rest. Her story was better than mine, so I had to step it up. I left my headlights shining green through those kiwis. All because Games was coming…but I wasn't."

Cherry laughed. Jake did, too. He knew the ending.

"The piano wire sank into the dark meat of that kid's throat like fishing line cracking through sunburned fingers at the end of the day. Maybe not fishing line. More like a finish line. And I'd strung his finish line on an angle so the wire would work with the speed of his Guinea racer and cut fast and deep. But the motherfucker's head stayed on! From up on the bridge, we saw his headlight flicker with the impact and I imagined those same hands that had stuffed my head in a toilet earlier that day wrestling with his own machine, maybe one hand coming up to keep his head on, too. Then he probably rode his bike to the ground, one hand still squeezing the gas, one hand squeezing the lawn sprinkler gushing from his throat. He might have made it another hundred feet, but the front wheel tangled around some weeds like spaghetti on a spoon—that's how dagoes eat that shit, you now—and there it stuck, him bleeding out, engine screaming like it knew what I did."

"Damn."

"When we ran up there, he must have still been alive because we saw his fingers just starting to loosen up—like when you spread them over a flashlight—and all that red came rushing out. The back wheel was still up and spinning, yearning for the road to get at me. And that screaming wheel was probably the last thing he heard, I guess. I tried to get in the headlight so he'd see me and know who won, but he was already gone. Hell, at least the bike knew."

...

What are you thinking?

Jake stands over the dead boys and their bikes. He strung guitar string through the corn maze where they raced and rode wheelies around the dead, muddy field, butting horns like rutting steers. Jakes' snares caught more than he'd hoped. He figures if he ties enough guitar string on the strongest stalks, or the tallest campaign crossbars, one day he'll snag the dirt bike who lanced his spokes and brought down his horse so easy. He just had to keep laying down more mouse traps.

More like bug strips, *he thought.*

But he doesn't know what to do with the rest of the day stretched out in front of him. Jake thinks about famous maniacs, the ones who left the body hanging or made half a snow angel or propped a victim up against some cryptic song lyric or left a head on the plastic Big Boy burger. Everyone always thinks that's a message. Not at all. They just didn't want to clean up. Maybe they were too bored to burn it or bury it or chop it up or even roll it in the water. Maybe the real nasty ones that get left all fucked up are just some nut going apeshit with the body because he's too lazy to start working.

The dirt bikes are as bent as the boys, necks still hanging on by some gristle, and Jake wonders if piano wire really is stronger. Not enough blood either. He flicks the exposed tendons and muscle on one boy with his steel-toe, catching a bundle of tissue like puppy scruff. Jake flinches when his boot makes the boy kick out a foot like a dog having nightmares. He heard once if you can grab the right wires, you could make a body talk, just like a dummy. And he's already proven that if you carry around a dead body and do the talking for it, your ventriloquism skills don't have to be top-notch with a corpse on the swing as a distraction.

"What are you thinking?"

Jake shudders to knock the question loose, then wonders if a bullet in the head would be as unimpressive as Cherry's own death at the doorway to a labyrinth of corn. One bullet, just a tiny black dot, the period at the end of the third-grade love letter she threw away, embarrassing to read even an hour after Jake wrote it.

Jake piggybacks Cherry back to the car, pulling her arms tighter around his neck. This Cherry talks even less than the Cherry that died here, but she's seen enough. She'd sleep on his shoulder everywhere now, even off the bike.

•••

"When we got up to the wreck, we couldn't make sense of what we were seeing. Maybe it was the shock of it all, but we couldn't tell where Games ended and the bike began..."

"Where the games ended!" Jake laughed.

"...and the color of the oil mixed with blood, what little we could see, didn't seem like blood at all. Once when I was a kid, I flipped backwards off the edge of my brother's—your dad's—new above-ground pool. And when I picked myself up off the grass, I found three white holes in my leg where the exposed bolts had punctured my shin. I ran to the house, expecting a gush down my leg any second, but even after a full five minutes, nothing. Just white holes. I panicked. I blacked out not because I'd popped three holes in my freakin' leg down to the freakin' bone, but because I thought I had nothing inside me. And I felt that same panic when we saw Games. Like we were made of shit that I knew nothin' about. But Cherry, she was panicking for other reasons, saying something about how tangled up he was with that motorcycle, his feet locked under the tailpipes, hands twisted behind his back and invisible. He was 'half boy, half bike,' she said. We were scared, sure. But something our dad—your grandpa—always said about killing a bug in your hand helped. If you squeeze it, it can bite, so remember to roll it in your fingers. That'll break it up easier than you ever knew. See, that's what we should have done with him, you know? So he wouldn't bite back. Get it?"

"Not really. Did you get in trouble?"

"Hell, no. Cherry ran first, and she started my panhead before I could climb on behind her. Yeah, behind her. Donkey style! She'd stolen my keys when I thought she was playing with my zipper. And we rode home, me with my head on her back this time, and I thought about her ghost story and the creature she'd made for me. Half bike, half boy. A green-eyed monster. A perfect centaur. With wings. And wheels..."

"Endgame," Jake said.

"Two childhood drawings combined," Cherry said.

"Your dad always hated that nickname," his uncle said. "But not as much as he hated you and me."

They sat in silence for about nine more swings.

"So, can I get that stuff from you, Jake?"

"Sure, Jake. Take whatever you need. All parts are interchangeable."

•••

Jake looks deep into the smoking hole where her mouth used to be. She doesn't know they're back at the scene of the crash where his wrecked bike slept unnoticed by traffic and patiently waiting for his return in the shade of a sign screaming "Hell Is Real!". He half-expects the bike to be teeming with noodles and rice, and he guns his shark past. He'd started the morning with a ghost story, even ate a spider so that nothing worse could happen to them all day, but he worries he should have eaten the frog instead when the rumble starts again and won't stop. He thinks of a warning from the dried-up 8-Ball, before the words got stuck on the window.

"You May Rely On It."

He takes a sharp turn and hears the echo of gutted guitars clanking around the Eldorado's trunk. He stomps some pedals. Then his brain is Jake Breaking again. Right in two.

•••

The two Jakes stood in the garage, somewhere on the border of morning and night. One said the other could take whatever he needed, and the other said pretty much the same thing.

Jake laid Cherry in the corner, near a pile of uprooted political posters, next to his uncle's Cherry, her dusty plastic head slumped to the side, puppet strings cut. He watched his uncle give him a look like, "That'll work," then bent down to give his girl a last kiss on the red Raggedy Anne apple of her face. His uncle's Cherry was a crash-test dummy who'd also served as a ballistics mannequin when she never showed damage after crashes at her old Kawasaki plant. This was before they brought in the new dummies, jam-packed with metal and electronics. Rotten fruit was smeared across her face, and paint chips framed the four-quadrant circle on her cheek, a yellow pie with two pieces gone. His uncle's Cherry had holes drilled in exactly three places, originally to gauge her impacts in the factory, later slathered with motor oil to become something else entirely. Her long, red hair slid off her head with a whisper when Jake picked her up, revealing the chipped jawbreaker of her skull. Uncle Jake thought about how most kids needed new models because of the upkeep. But his nephew was raised better than that.

Jake ducked under the door with the mannequin in his arms, smiling at the weight, smiling at how easily things were replaced, nuzzling the wear and tear, the history on her face, already wondering what she's thinking. Her head lolled off his shoulder, and he shook her like a baby, hearing the heavy rattle deep in her belly. He wasn't sure if he could pull his uncle's gun from her mouth or between her legs. Both seemed impossible. He put her on his back.

Then he went for the pile of smashed Alamo guitars and started loading them in the Eldorado's trunk. He drove away with her head on his shoulder, listening to new stories.

Back in the garage, Jake's engine rumbled, and the sweet fog of exhaust smoke billowed around his knees. Everything rumbled. Rumbling was a tradition in their family. Just like 8-balls. And he collected both, acrylic and "magic." Both Jakes knew the magic ones were full of alcohol, having cracked open dozens to get drunk on special occasions. Like tonight.

Uncle Jake turned his new Cherry's head around so she couldn't watch, careful not to slip a finger into the yawning void at the base of her fractured skull. Then he stood up straight in the mirrored chrome of the hardtail fender and put on his uniform.

He pulled leather chaps over his ratty jeans, snapped and buckled and zipped and zipped. Chains rattled and gloves squeaked, and his boots scuffed half-moons around his motorcycle in anticipation. He swapped out his Highland High jacket for Douches Wild, stinking to high heaven of gasoline and mothballs. He reached into the front pocket, flicking away an empty pack of Beeman's and gathering up a slick, heavy wad of Socony 990 that had pooled there. Checking his face in the fender, he streaked his grey hair black, finished buttoning up the jacket with the reverence of a wedding tux, then with one last hand through his widow's peak, got down on his knees and mounted the bike from behind.

Even though they would have been great to grip, he was relieved they weren't old enough for saddle bags. And as he unzipped his fly and squeezed his shit until the end got red and angry and mushroomed in his fist, he coughed a swirl of sweet carbon monoxide and laughed. He remembered all her nicknames, once "Hardly Driveable," but now a genuine "Hogly Ferguson" if he ever saw one.

He greased the edge of the tailpipe with the rest of his oily palms, and jammed it in. The pipes were made skinny back then, so the hot metal pinched the head, sizzling all around the purple helmet, crackling on the chrome plating, burning fast to resist his thrusts. He bit his tongue and pushed harder, fucking her hoggy style, smelling the old scars on his meat crackle like bacon, scraping rust flakes into his white bush like tinsel on a sagging tree with every stroke.

The bike idled high, and the rockers on the V-twin boogied until they blurred. But Jake could still see his reflection in them and mumbled something about bikes and bopping being a way of life. Then he wondered if a cooling ring on the exhaust would keep him hard longer. Then his vision got hazy in the fumes, and he imagined something about hogs trying to buck him off. The engine revved, and Jake looked up at the throttle where he swore he saw his brother hang his helmet on the handlebars, a helmet with his head still smiling inside. His lips now cherry-red, Jake fucked the bike harder as he worried his brother Rusty, head be damned, had been banging her when he wasn't around.

He pushed harder and felt his scorched foreskin stuck tight, then peel back even further, layer after layer, until he half-prolapsed like a tube sock stuck on a toe and rolled inside out. The hot pipe had finally opened his urethra so wide he'd become one with the motorcycle, sharing the same heart, lungs, regulator, and now, exhaust system. She pumped her hot smoke deep into his bladder, deeper into his balls, filling his body with the lifeblood of a machine.

ACKNOWLEDGEMENTS

On July 27, 2013, I finished proofing the print copy of *Hoods, Hot Rods, and Hellcats*. When I was done I sent the small list of corrections to Brian Roe. The next day, on Facebook, I read that Mick Farren had died after collapsing onstage at the Borderline Club in London, where he was performing as part of the Atomic Sunshine Festival.

The news floored me.

Farren was one of my idols and kind enough to write this introduction. I felt like I owed him something more substantial in these acknowledgments. A reminiscence about my first time reading *The Quest Of The DNA Cowboys* or *Their Master's War*. A short essay on your responsibilities as a human being and as an artist, especially in regards to our current sociopolitical climate, maybe opening with that Brecht quote about how the worst illiterate is a political illiterate. Or even a rafter-shaking rant about how the only word I hate more than "noir" is "transgressive" because at least noir means black in French and French is a damn pretty language, but transgressive is an ugly word used to market fiction that's actually about as transgressive as when you stole your dad's cigarettes in junior high and told dead baby jokes on the school bus.

But no, I think the best thing to do for Mick is stick with what I originally wrote...

"I did it alone" is a pervasive and evil myth that twists our understanding of what it means to share the planet with 7 billion other humans, it's a lingering part of the Alger Infection still eating at America's rotting carcass. So take a minute and prepare yourself for this bit of news...we are all in this together. Society could not function otherwise. We would not be here today if it ever had—the saber-toothed cats would have eaten us before we ever stopped dragging our knuckles and scratching our heads trying to figure out that farming thing.

My name is on the front cover, but what you hold in your hands? I certainly did not do this alone. You would not have this book were it not for: my wife's unquestionable support, my idol's gracious introduction, Garnett Elliott and Thomas Pluck shaping my story into something other than a dialogue-heavy mess, Skott Kilander providing fantastic cover art, Curtis Pierce giving us some cool interior illustrations, Brian Roe designing the classy print edition, Chris Hosler checking all our facts, and

Jaye Manus demonstrating her e-book mastery. Not to mention Tyler Andrews, Vanessa Lopa, and Rubi Kayobi all donating their prodigious talents to the Indiegogo campaign.

Life doesn't care about our plans any more than it cares about our desires. This truth was never clearer for me than when I tried to bring this anthology to fruition. Only one thing exceeds the immense talent of everyone involved in this project.

Their patience.

~Chad Eagleton

CONTRIBUTORS

Eric Beetner, winner of the 2012 Stalker Award for Most Criminally Underrated Author, is the author of *The Devil Doesn't Want Me*, *Dig Two Graves* and the story collection *A Bouquet of Bullets*. He is co-author (with JB Kohl) of *One Too Many Blows To The Head* and the sequel, *Borrowed Trouble*, as well as writing two novellas in the acclaimed Fightcard series, *Split Decision* and *A Mouth Full Of Blood*. His award-winning short stories have appeared in over a dozen anthologies. Visit him at ericbeetner.blogspot.com.

Chad Eagleton is a two time Watery Grave Invitational finalist. His story "Ghostman on Third" was nominated for the Spinetingler Award. His fiction is available in print and e-book, as well as online at such sites as *A Twist of Noir*, *Bad Things*, *The Pulp Pusher*, *Beat To A Pulp*, *Darkness Before the Dawn*, and *Shotgun Honey*.

Mick Farren was an English author, poet, critic, musician, activist, and counter-culture icon. He fronted the anarchic pre-punk band The Deviants and his lyrics have been recorded by Metallica, Motörhead, Hawkwind, Brother Wayne Kramer, and the Pink Fairies. His twenty-two novels range from the psychedelic fantasy of The DNA Cowboys Trilogy to the neo-gothic The Renquist Quartet. He published more than a dozen non-fiction works on drugs, conspiracy theory, popular culture, and Elvis Presley before departing this dimension for parts unknown.

Matthew Funk is an editor of *Needle Magazine* and a staff writer for *Planet Fury* and *Criminal Complex*. Winner of the 2010 Spinetingler Award for Best Short Story on the Web, Funk has work in print and at numerous Web sites, indexed on his Web domain.

Christopher Grant is the editor and publisher of *A Twist Of Noir* (a-twist-of-noir. blogspot.com). He is also a writer of crime/noir, bizarro and various other things.

David James Keaton's fiction has appeared or is forthcoming in *Horror Factory*, *Noir At The Bar 2*, and *Uncle B's Drive-In Fiction*, among others. He received a 2012 Spinetingler Award for his contribution to *Crime Factory #8*, and his coach-killing fantasy in *Plots With Guns #10* was named a Notable Story of 2010 by *storySouth's* Million Writer's Award. His collection *FISH BITES COP! Stories To Bash Authorities* (Comet Press) is due out in early 2013. He can currently be found at davidjameskeaton.com, flywheelmag.com, or in Kentucky, where he watches dozens of motorcycles hang out at the gas station behind his house. They have colorful lights all over them these days and look straight out of *Tron*.

Skott Kilander survived a Midwestern American upbringing, dropped out of college, met a girl, and moved...somewhere else in the Midwest. He resides in Pennsylvania with his lovely wife and daughter, where he obsesses over vintage pulp covers and teaching himself to paint better. Artwork and self-deprecating commentary can be found at sleepyoni.blogspot.com.

Nik Korpon is the author of *Old Ghosts, By the Nails of the Warpriest* and the collection *Bar Scars*. His stories have blackened the eyes of *Needle Magazine, Beat to a Pulp: Hardboiled, Shotgun Honey, Warmed and Bound: A Velvet Anthology, Speedloader* and a bunch more, and have been nominated for a couple awards for some unknown reason. He lives in Baltimore with his wife and son. Give him some danger, little stranger, at nikkorpon.com.

Heath Lowrance is the author of *City of Heretics, The Bastard Hand, Dig Ten Graves*, and the "Hawthorne" series of weird western stories. He's been a movie theater manager, a tour guide at Sun Studio, and a singer in a punk band. He lives in Lansing, Michigan, with his wife.

Curtis A. Pierce lives in Indianapolis, Indiana. He spent 5 years studying at Vincennes University's Art Program, and Herron School of Art. Currently, he is a tattoo artist at The Rue Morgue Tattoo Gallery in Shelbyville, Indiana. He is also a freelance prismacolor artist and painter when not creating custom tattoos for the masses.

Thomas Pluck writes unflinching fiction with heart. His stories have appeared in *Shotgun Honey, PANK magazine, Crime Factory, Spinetingler, Plots with Guns, Beat to a Pulp, McSweeney's, The Utne Reader* and elsewhere. He edits the *Lost Children* charity anthologies to benefit The National Association to Protect Children. He is working on his first novel. He lives in New Jersey with his wife Sarah. You can find him as @tommysalami on Twitter, and on the web at www.thomaspluck.com.

Brian S. Roe is s a native of Indianapolis, Indiana, and a graduate of the Herron School of Art and Design. He is a partner in RSquared Studios, a production and publishing company for comic books and tabletop games. He writes the comics *Zombie Plague, Yva Starling: Troubleshooter* and the forthcoming *Tiki Tribe versus Cthulhu Cult*.